Digital Love, Analog Hearts

Bangalore's Crime Riddle

Sneha Sreekumar

Ukiyoto Publishing

All global publishing rights are held by

Ukiyoto Publishing

Published in 2023

Content Copyright © Sneha Sreekumar

ISBN 9789360494445

All rights reserved.
No part of this publication may be reproduced, transmitted, or stored in a retrieval system, in any form by any means, electronic, mechanical, photocopying, recording or otherwise, without the prior permission of the publisher.

The moral rights of the author have been asserted.

This is a work of fiction. Names, characters, businesses, places, events, locales, and incidents are either the products of the author's imagination or used in a fictitious manner. Any resemblance to actual persons, living or dead, or actual events is purely coincidental

This book is sold subject to the condition that it shall not by way of trade or otherwise, be lent, resold, hired out or otherwise circulated, without the publisher's prior consent, in any form of binding or cover other than that in which it is published.

www.ukiyoto.com

Dedication

To my dearest Amma, Acha, & Unni,

This book is a tribute to you, the unwavering pillars of my life's journey. With every word I've written in this book, I find a piece of each of you. Acha - Your innate talent for weaving words into vivid tapestries has been my guiding light, a legacy I carry with pride and joy. Thank you for entrusting me with this precious gift of writing, a bond we uniquely share and a gift I cherish with every breath. Amma & Unni - Your enthusiasm for delving into each piece I pen has been the sweetest melody to my writer's soul. It has been the best encouragement ever! Your voices, always filled with excitement and pride, have echoed in my heart, pushing me to reach new heights with my pen. This first work of mine is a dedication to you, who have been my guiding stars at every step, supporting me and believing in me even when I doubted myself.

To the love of my life - My dear husband, and the love of our life - Our little Shresht,

You have been the serene sanctuary amidst the whirlwind of my creativity. In the beautiful chaos of my creative world and the storm of my imagination, you've been the pillars of peace and understanding. Your support, the quiet evenings and nights when you've allowed me to lose myself in writing, have been the foundation on which this dream was built. Every word here is infused with the love and space you've given me to let my thoughts and creativity take flight. You've been the wind beneath my wings, and for that, I am eternally grateful.

Finally, this dedication extends to my entire circle of family, extended family, and friends. Each one of you, too numerous to name but equally cherished, has played a crucial role in my journey as a writer.

Your kind words, enthusiasm for my posts, and words of encouragement have been the brushstrokes on the canvas of my writing journey. Your belief in my talent has been a constant source of motivation to improve and evolve.

To all of you, this book is a manifestation of your faith in me, a dream turned into reality through the love and support you've generously given. Thank you for being a part of my story.

With a heart full of love, gratitude, and emotions that words can barely capture,
Sneha Sreekumar

Preface

I have been lost in thought, pondering how to introduce you to the world I've created in "Digital Love, Analog Hearts: Bangalore's Crime Riddle." You see, this book is a little piece of my heart and soul, a blend of my fascination with the intricate web of cybercrimes and my love for storytelling, something I owe largely to Bollywood.

I have named the protagonists in my story Anjali Sharma & Rahul Nair. Why Anjali and Rahul? Well, if you've ever lost yourself in the captivating world of Bollywood, especially in Karan Johar's movies, you'll know the magic these names hold. They remind me of rainy evenings spent watching vibrant stories unfold on the screen, stories that made me laugh, cry, and dream. So, when I was creating my protagonists, I couldn't think of any names more fitting than these, which have become synonymous with friendship, love, and a bit of drama.

This book isn't just about the cyber mysteries of Bangalore, a city that I've grown to love and understand. It's also about the people who live in this world. Anjali and Rahul's journey through the maze of high-tech crimes is also a journey of understanding each other and themselves. It's about finding human connections in a digital world that can sometimes feel isolating.

Writing this story was like piecing together a puzzle. I delved into the world of cybersecurity, a topic that both daunts and intrigues many of us. But, as I wove the tale, I realized it was the human element that fascinated me the most – the stories behind the screens, the decisions, the dilemmas, the raw emotions.

In a way, "Digital Love, Analog Hearts" is my homage to the films that shaped my understanding of storytelling. It's a tale where technology meets emotions, where Anjali and Rahul not only chase cyber villains but also grapple with the very human issues of trust, friendship, and maybe a little more.

So, as you turn these pages, I invite you to join me in a story that's a blend of thrill, drama, and heartfelt moments. This is my first novel, and it's as real and personal as it gets – a tale of modern crimes and timeless emotions, a narrative where each character and turn might surprise you, just as they surprised me while writing.

Thank you for picking up my book, and I hope you find a little piece of yourself in this story, just as I have.

Contents

Introduction	1
Prologue	3
Anjali's Discovery	5
Rahul's Enigma	11
First Encounter	15
Alliance of Necessity	21
Chasing Shadows	30
Unseen Connections	39
Tangled Webs	48
Conflicting Emotions	66
Uncharted Waters	74
Bonds Tested	82
Shadows Lifted	89
The Final Confrontation	94
New Beginnings	98
Epilogue: To Love, Laughter & Happily Ever After..!!!	107
About the Author	*110*

Introduction

Welcome to my very first venture into storytelling. In this novel, "Digital Love, Analog Hearts: Bangalore's Crime Riddle," I invite you to explore the vibrant and tech-driven streets of Bangalore, a city that's as rich in history as it is in innovation.

At the heart of this tale are two intriguing characters: Anjali Sharma, a journalist with a fierce passion for truth, and Rahul Nair, a cybersecurity expert with a hidden past. Together, they find themselves entangled in a web of cybercrimes that challenge the safety and ethics of the digital world they inhabit.

This story is much more than a mere mystery; it's a narrative about the resilience of the human spirit and the unlikely bonds that form under pressure. As a first-time author, I aimed to craft a tale that is both thrilling and heartfelt, capturing the essence of Bangalore — a city of contrasts, where ancient traditions seamlessly blend with the rush of modern technology.

As Anjali and Rahul unravel complex digital puzzles, they also embark on personal journeys of growth and discovery. Their initial reluctance to work together slowly transforms into a deep, collaborative partnership, mirroring the unpredictable nature of life itself.

I penned this novel with the hope of offering you, the reader, a window into a world where technology intersects with human emotions, where every clue leads to new revelations, and where the heart finds its strength amidst chaos.

So, come along on this adventure through the bustling lanes and hidden corners of Bangalore. Discover with Anjali and Rahul the fine lines between right and wrong in the digital age, and experience the joy of uncovering mysteries that lie just beneath the surface of our tech-savvy world.

Thank you for joining me on this exciting new journey. I hope this story resonates with you as much as it has with me while writing it.

Prologue

In the enchanting twilight, Bangalore, known as the Garden City, was bathed in a serene glow. Its skyline stood in stark silhouette against the deep blue sky. Amidst this urban landscape, famous for its sprawling tech parks, an unassuming building buzzed with unexpected activity.

The scene shifts inside to a dimly lit room, where the only sources of light are the flickering screens of numerous computers. Here, a solitary figure is engrossed in their work, their fingers moving rapidly over a keyboard. They are engrossed in a task far from ordinary—a digital age heist. The computer screen in front of them is alive with rapidly scrolling code, too fast for the eye to catch.

This hacker, a shadowy figure in the world of cyber anonymity, is infiltrating one of Bangalore's major financial institutions. They expertly dismantle the digital defences, each falling like dominoes in a well-planned sequence. The only light in the room is the harsh, blue glow of the computer screen, which illuminates the hacker's face, a portrait of intense focus.

Outside, the bustling city remains unaware of the drama unfolding within its digital framework. Life continues as usual—cars navigate the streets, people engage in evening activities, and the stars begin to dot the sky, all oblivious to the digital shadow creeping through the city's technological core.

Back inside, the hacker is close to their goal. With a few final keystrokes, they breach the heart of the financial database. Sensitive information is now at their fingertips: account numbers, transaction histories, and personal data, all vulnerable and waiting to be exploited.

But then, an unexpected message flashes on the screen, a simple line of text that sends a wave of cold fear through the hacker: "You are not alone." This message disrupts the rhythm of their operation, planting seeds of doubt and fear. Had they been detected? Was this a trap? The room, once a sanctuary for their unlawful mission, now feels like a trap. The walls seem to close in, and the once-promising glow of the screens now signals potential doom.

In the heart of Bangalore, a tense and unpredictable game of cat and mouse has just begun.

Anjali's Discovery

In the heart of Bangalore, amidst the towering glass buildings and bustling streets, lay the office of 'The Bangalore Beat'. It was in this hive of activity where Anjali, a journalist par excellence, found her calling. The newsroom was a mosaic of chaos and creativity, a place where stories were born and truths unearthed. The incessant clatter of keyboards, the intermittent chime of phones, and the sporadic bursts of conversation created a symphony that was music to Anjali's ears. Here, amidst the chaos, she thrived, her mind always in pursuit of the next big story.

Anjali hailed from a small, picturesque town in the lush landscapes of Karnataka. Growing up in a family where education and knowledge were revered, her childhood was steeped in a rich tapestry of stories and learning. Her father, a local school teacher, and her mother, a devoted homemaker who loved literature, instilled in her a profound respect for the power of words and narratives. Her home was a treasure trove of books, ranging from ancient epics to contemporary literature, fostering in her an insatiable curiosity about the world and its myriad stories.

During her teenage years, Anjali's family moved to Bangalore, seeking better educational opportunities for her and her siblings. The transition from a small town to a bustling metropolis was a culture shock for young Anjali, but it also opened her eyes to the diverse tapestry of life and the multitude of stories waiting to be told. She quickly adapted to her new environment, her keen observation skills and natural empathy helping her connect with people from all walks of life.

Journalism happened to Anjali almost by serendipity. Initially interested in literature and creative writing, she discovered her true passion during her college years when she joined the university newspaper. The thrill of investigative journalism, the rush of chasing stories, and the satisfaction of shedding light on untold narratives resonated deeply with her. She realized that journalism was not just a profession but a calling – a way to make an impact, to give voice to the voiceless, and to bring truth to the forefront.

After completing her education, Anjali's talent and drive led her to 'The Bangalore Beat', where she quickly made a name for herself. Her sharp eyes, always observing and probing, could spot the most elusive details, akin to finding a needle in a haystack. Her instincts, honed by years of navigating the complex layers of stories, were unparalleled in the world of journalism.

Physically, Anjali was a striking figure. Her medium height was complemented by a poised, confident demeanour. Her long, dark hair, often pulled back in a practical bun while working, framed a face that was both intelligent and expressive. Her eyes, a deep shade of brown, were windows to a mind that was always analyzing, always questioning. Anjali's choice of attire was simple yet elegant, often a blend of traditional Indian and comfortable Western wear, reflecting her grounded yet adaptable personality. Anjali was a force to be reckoned with. Her sharp eyes could spot the needle in the haystack, and her instincts were unparalleled in the world of journalism.

At her desk, which served as more of a strategic command centre, she was surrounded by mountains of papers, each a piece of the intricate puzzle she was solving. Multiple cups of half-drunk coffee stood testament to the hours she had spent working. Her computer screen, aglow with a collage of open tabs, articles, data sheets, and police reports, was a reflection of her diligent search for the truth.

The story that had ensnared Anjali's attention began as a series of cybercrimes, each unique in method but uniform in audacity and precision. The targets were diverse – a prominent bank, a rising tech company, and even a government office had fallen victim. Each had been hacked with such sophistication that they left no trace of the perpetrators. The police, baffled, had chalked them up to isolated incidents by different groups. But Anjali, with her keen sense of pattern recognition, saw something else – a thread that connected these disparate events.

Her fingers danced over the keyboard, each stroke bringing her closer to unravelling this mystery. Memories of her conversation with Inspector Prakash from the cybercrime unit lingered in her mind. He had dismissed her theories, attributing the crimes to the city's numerous tech-savvy individuals. But Anjali wasn't convinced. The variation in targets and the diversity in methods pointed to something more orchestrated, a pattern too intricate to be coincidental.

As she delved deeper, her phone rang, jolting her from her thoughts. It was Tina, her colleague and closest confidante in the newsroom. Tina's voice, a blend of concern and curiosity, inquired about Anjali's latest obsession. Despite Tina's subtle warnings about the potential dangers of her investigation, Anjali remained undeterred. She was sure that there was a sophisticated and significant pattern to these attacks, a conviction she voiced with unwavering certainty.

The day aged into the evening, and the bustling energy of the newsroom gradually waned. Yet, Anjali remained, her gaze locked onto her screen, her mind tirelessly piecing together the complex puzzle. And then, in a moment of epiphany, she noticed it – a minuscule, almost imperceptible detail in the code used in one of the hacks. It was a signature style she had encountered before in a different cybercrime. To an untrained eye, it would have gone unnoticed, but not to Anjali.

Her heart raced with excitement. This was the breakthrough she had been waiting for. The discovery that these crimes, seemingly the work of multiple hackers, were the machinations of one person or a single group. This revelation hinted at a conspiracy far more significant than anyone had anticipated.

Anjali leaned back in her chair, her mind a whirlwind of questions and theories. Who was behind these meticulously planned attacks? What was their endgame? The depth of this rabbit hole was yet unknown, but Anjali was determined to explore its every corner.

She grabbed her notepad and pen, her indispensable tools, and began to strategize her next moves. Her investigation would start with the tech companies. She planned to comb through their records, scrutinize their employee lists, and chase down every lead. Somewhere within the labyrinth of data and names lay the key to unravelling this enigma.

As she stepped out of the now-deserted newsroom, the weight of the impending night did nothing to dampen her resolve. Her eyes, fierce with determination, reflected a determination to uncover a story that had the potential to shake the very core of Bangalore's prestigious tech industry.

But this story was more than a simple investigation. It was a journey that would plunge Anjali into a world brimming with peril, riddles, and unexpected alliances. She was about to tread a path that would challenge her convictions and force her to confront the shadows that lurked behind the screens of the digital age. This was just the beginning of a saga that would test her every belief, a story that would etch her name in the annals of journalistic excellence. Anjali's quest for the truth had led her to the precipice of a revelation that would change not just her life but the entire landscape of cybercrime in the city.

As she walked into the cool Bangalore night, her silhouette merged with the shadows, and Anjali was unaware of the twists and turns that lay ahead. But one thing was certain – she was ready for whatever lay ahead, armed with her sharp mind, unwavering spirit, and an unquenchable thirst for the truth. The story of Anjali's discovery was just beginning, a tale that would unfold in the pages of 'The Bangalore Beat,' capturing the imagination of its readers and etching a permanent mark in the world of journalism.

Rahul's Enigma

In the bustling epicenter of Bangalore's tech district, where the skyline was a mosaic of architectural marvels and technological prowess, stood the impressive edifice of SecureTech Solutions. Its glass facade glinted in the sun, symbolizing the city's burgeoning tech industry. On the fifteenth floor, in a corner office that commanded a panoramic view of the urban tapestry below, Rahul Nair, the lead cybersecurity analyst of SecureTech, was engrossed in his digital domain.

The office was a sanctuary of high-tech equipment and the latest cybersecurity tools. Three large monitors formed an arc on Rahul's desk, each displaying streams of code and complex data visualizations. His laptop, stationed in the middle, was the epicentre of his operations, its keys worn out from the intensity of his daily endeavours. The room buzzed with controlled chaos, reflecting the constant battle waged against cyber threats.

Rahul's team, a group of carefully selected individuals, each an expert in their respective fields, worked in a harmonious frenzy. Amidst this whirlwind of activity, Aman, a young but incredibly talented team member, called out to Rahul about an anomaly detected in the server logs. Rahul, his fingers a blur on the keyboard, seamlessly transitioned his focus to the new challenge. To him, these moments were not merely occupational hazards but the very essence of his passion – the thrill of unravelling mysteries that lurked in the depths of cyberspace.

However, beneath Rahul's composed and focused exterior lay a complex and shadowed past. His dark eyes, usually brimming with intelligence and determination, sometimes betrayed hints of this hidden history. Only a select few knew of the life Rahul had led before he became a beacon of cybersecurity – a life marked by rebellious exploits in the digital underworld.

On this particular day, as Rahul navigated through the labyrinth of digital information, a news alert from 'The Bangalore Beat' caught his attention. The article detailed the latest in a string of sophisticated cybercrimes plaguing the city. Something in the report struck a chord in Rahul – a fleeting expression of recognition, perhaps concern, crossed his face. Aman, ever observant, noticed this rare crack in Rahul's armour and voiced his concern. Rahul's response, a mix of humour and evasion, did little to reveal the storm of thoughts brewing within him.

The evening unfolded with Rahul and his team engrossed in their digital battle. They skillfully contained the anomaly, adding another notch to their long list of victories against the unseen adversaries of the digital world. As the office gradually emptied, Rahul remained, his mind replaying the news about the cybercrimes. There was an unsettling familiarity about them, a distant echo from a past he had tried to leave behind.

Rahul's journey to this point had been unconventional. Once a maverick hacker known for his audacious exploits in the virtual world, he had chosen to leave that life behind. He transformed himself, using his exceptional skills for the greater good. Yet, the shadows of his former life lingered beneath the surface of his new identity, occasionally surfacing in moments of introspection.

Standing up, Rahul stretched his tall, athletic frame and walked to the large window. The view from his office was spectacular – the city lights of Bangalore twinkled like stars in a vast urban cosmos. It was here, in this city, that Rahul had sought redemption and a fresh start. He had found a semblance of peace and a sense of purpose in his role at SecureTech. However, the recent spate of cybercrimes stirred a sense of disquiet in him, reminding him of the world he had left behind but which had never truly let go of him.

With a deep, contemplative sigh, Rahul turned away from the window. The office, now silent and devoid of its usual energy, seemed like a different world. He picked up his jacket and began to walk through the deserted corridors. His footsteps echoed in the stillness, a solitary reminder of his isolation amidst the crowd. In this moment of solitude, Rahul made a decision – he would keep an eye on the developments of these cybercrimes, observing from a distance. He understood that the past had a way of catching up, no matter how hard one tried to outrun it.

Unknown to Rahul, his path was destined to intertwine with that of Anjali, a journalist whose tenacity and pursuit of truth would draw him into a vortex of events beyond his anticipation. This convergence would not only compel him to confront the ghosts of his past but also challenge his understanding of himself and the world he inhabited. His decision to monitor the cybercrimes would set in motion a series of events, intertwining his fate with Anjali's in a narrative brimming with intrigue, danger, and revelations. As Rahul walked through the quiet hallways of SecureTech, he was oblivious to the fact that he was stepping into a chapter of his life that would redefine his existence and test the very foundations of his beliefs.

First Encounter

As dawn broke over Bangalore, painting the sky in hues of gold and amber, the city stirred to life, pulsating with the unyielding rhythm of progress and daily bustle. Amidst this lively backdrop, Anjali Sharma, a distinguished journalist from 'The Bangalore Beat,' stood at the entrance of SecureTech Solutions. She was a striking figure, draped in a long, red kurta that spoke of her boldness and vitality. The vibrant colour mirrored her fiery dedication, making her stand out amid the city's corporate landscape.

Anjali's kurta, adorned with intricate patterns, fluttered gently in the morning breeze as if echoing her restless spirit. Her attire was not just a choice of fashion but a reflection of her identity – a blend of traditional grace and unyielding tenacity. Each fold of the fabric seemed to tell a story, a narrative of the countless stories she had chased down in her career.

Her eyes, large and brimming with questions, scanned the world around her with a curiosity that had driven her through countless stories and investigations. They sparkled with intelligence and intensity that bespoke a mind always at work, dissecting and analyzing the world in search of hidden truths. These were the eyes of a seeker, ever vigilant and unafraid to gaze into the heart of complex narratives.

Anjali's hair, long and unrestrained, cascaded down her shoulders in a flow of ebony waves. It swayed with each step she took, a testament to her free-spirited approach to life and work. Her hair was not merely an aspect of her appearance; it was a symbol of her refusal to be confined by the expectations and norms that often bound others. It represented her independence, a flag of rebellion against the conventional, mirroring the fearless spirit with which she approached her journalism.

Anjali's arrival at SecureTech Solutions was the culmination of a series of meticulously planned steps, propelled by her investigative instincts and a deep-seated determination to unravel a complex web of cybercrimes that had recently plagued Bangalore. Her journey to SecureTech was not just a physical traversal through the city but also a strategic move in her investigative process, one that she hoped would bring her closer to the elusive truth.

Anjali's interest in the series of cybercrimes had been piqued initially by their precision and audacity. The targets were diverse – from high-profile banks to emerging tech companies and government offices – each victimized in a manner that was both sophisticated and untraceable. The local police had been quick to dismiss these as isolated incidents, but Anjali, known for her sharp analytical skills and her ability to see patterns where others saw chaos, suspected a deeper connection.

Driven by a relentless pursuit of the truth, Anjali had embarked on an exhaustive investigation. She spent hours at her desk at 'The Bangalore Beat,' poring over reports, connecting dots, and reaching out to her extensive network of contacts for leads. Her investigation led her to believe that the key to understanding these cybercrimes lay in understanding their methods – the digital fingerprints left behind by the perpetrators. The breakthrough came when Anjali identified a pattern in the coding anomalies used in the cyberattacks, a signature style that pointed toward a sophisticated level of expertise in cybersecurity. This revelation led her to SecureTech Solutions, a renowned firm in the city known for its cutting-edge work in cybersecurity and digital forensics.

Anjali's decision to visit SecureTech was twofold. Firstly, she hoped to gain technical insights into the cyberattacks, to understand the complexities of the methods used. She believed that speaking with experts in the field would provide her with the technical grounding she needed to further her investigation. Secondly, and more importantly, she suspected that SecureTech, being at the forefront of cybersecurity in Bangalore, might unknowingly hold clues or connections to the individuals or groups behind the cyberattacks.

Entering SecureTech Solutions, Anjali felt the transition from the chaotic energy of Bangalore's streets to the controlled, almost sterile atmosphere of the corporate world. She moved with purposeful grace, her red kurta contrasting sharply against the sleek, modern aesthetics of the building. The receptionist led her through a series of corridors, each turn bringing her closer to the epicentre of the cybersecurity storm she was determined to understand.

In a conference room bathed in the soft glow of morning light, Rahul, the lead cybersecurity analyst at SecureTech, awaited her. He stood as she entered, his height and stature imposing, yet it was Anjali who commanded the space. Her presence was a vibrant splash of colour and life in the monochrome setting. Her eyes, wide with an insatiable thirst for knowledge, met his with unflinching directness.

"Anjali Sharma from 'The Bangalore Beat,'" she announced, her voice resonating with confidence honed through years of journalistic pursuits. She extended her hand, firm and assured.

"Please, call me Rahul," he responded his tone a mix of professional courtesy and a hint of intrigue. The contrast between them was striking – his guarded demeanour and her open, inquisitive presence.

As they sat, the room seemed to shrink in the face of Anjali's personality. Her red kurta was not just a garment but a banner of her passion for uncovering the truth. She opened her notepad, each page a battleground of past journalistic victories and challenges.

The interview began, with Anjali steering the conversation with the skill of an experienced journalist.

Her questions were like arrows, aimed precisely at unravelling the mystery of the cybercrimes. Rahul, in turn, responded with guarded precision, clearly aware that he was dealing with a mind as sharp as his own.

Anjali probed deeper, her big eyes unblinking, reflecting a mind that was piecing together the puzzle before her. Rahul found himself caught in her gaze, challenged and intrigued by the depth of her inquiries. He navigated her questions with care, aware of the keen intellect he was engaging with.

Their discussion was a dance of words and wits, a meeting of two minds both seeking the truth, albeit from different perspectives. Anjali's red kurta seemed to glow brighter with each question she posed, a visual echo of her growing intrigue and determination.

As the meeting drew to a close, Rahul stood, extending his hand once more. His words of caution to Anjali were tinged with newfound respect. "Good luck with your investigation, Ms. Sharma. But remember, the digital world is a labyrinth."

Anjali rose, her kurta swaying, her hair a fluid shadow of her movements. She met his gaze squarely, a spark of challenge in her eyes. "I've always been good at navigating labyrinths," she replied, her voice a blend of confidence and anticipation.

Stepping out of SecureTech, Anjali was a vivid image against the backdrop of the city's corporate greys. The streets of Bangalore welcomed her back, her red kurta a flame moving through the currents of the city. She left behind a lasting impression, a reminder that she was not just a journalist but a force of nature – unyielding, vibrant, and relentless in her quest for truth.

As she made her way through the city, Anjali's mind raced with thoughts and theories. Rahul had been a revelation – a character with depths she was eager to explore. She sensed that their encounter was the beginning of a journey that would lead her down paths filled with revelations and dangers alike.

Unaware of the twists her story was yet to take, Anjali moved through Bangalore, her red kurta a symbol of her spirit, her eyes alight with the promise of discovery. This was more than just a story; it was an odyssey that would test her limits and reveal the layers of a city ensnared in digital intrigue. Anjali was on the verge of uncovering a narrative that would resonate far beyond the confines of 'The Bangalore Beat,' a story that would intertwine her fate with Rahul's in ways she could not yet foresee.

In the days to come, as she delved deeper into the cyber mystery, the image of her in the red kurta, with questioning eyes and free-flowing hair, would become a symbol of her journey – a journey into the heart of the digital age, where secrets lay hidden and truths were waiting to be unearthed.

Alliance of Necessity

The evening descended upon Bangalore like a mystical shroud, draping the city in shades of twilight. As the sun dipped below the horizon, its final rays cast elongated shadows across the bustling streets, creating a contrast of light and dark that mirrored the duality of the city itself. Amid this transition, Anjali, known for her unwavering tenacity, traversed the lesser-known alleys of Bangalore. Her day had been a whirlwind – a series of interviews, relentless pursuit of leads, and the meticulous assembly of the fragmented pieces of a complex story that was slowly coming to life under her scrutiny.

The alleyway she chose deviated from her customary path, a decision guided by intuition and a desire for reflection. Here, away from the cacophony of the city, the atmosphere was eerily tranquil. The alley, with its weathered buildings and walls adorned with layers of graffiti, spoke of forgotten stories and hidden truths. Anjali's steps echoed on the worn pavement, each footfall punctuation in her train of thought, as she dissected the day's events, unaware of the lurking shadow in the periphery.

Abruptly, the quietude was shattered. A figure detached itself from the shadows, an ominous presence that moved with a predatory swiftness. Anjali's heart raced, her instincts as a reporter instantly recognizing the imminent danger. The silhouette advanced, the faint glimmer of metal in his hand visible in the subdued light, signalling a threat that was all too real.

In that split second, where instinct and fear collided, another figure intervened. With a burst of speed and force, he crashed into the assailant. Anjali stumbled back, her mind grappling with the rapid unfolding of events. It was Rahul – the cybersecurity analyst from SecureTech Solutions – his face etched with fierce determination as he engaged in a physical struggle with the attacker.

The confrontation was intense and swift. Rahul's movements were precise, a testament to skills not often associated with a cybersecurity expert. His agility and strength overwhelmed the assailant, who, realizing the futility of his attack, retreated hastily into the darkness.

Panting from the exertion, Rahul turned to Anjali, his expression softening from combative resolve to concern, though a trace of anger still flickered in his eyes. "Are you alright?" he asked, his voice laden with a mixture of relief and apprehension.

Anjali, her pulse still racing, managed a nod. "Yes, I'm fine. But why... how did you happen to be here?" Rahul averted his gaze momentarily before answering, "I've been keeping an eye on you. Your investigation... I suspected it might put you in danger." A maelstrom of emotions and questions whirled within Anjali. "Why would anyone target me? And why are you, of all people, following me?"

Rahul's eyes met hers, revealing a sincerity she hadn't seen during their previous encounters. "The story you're pursuing is much bigger and more perilous than you realize. There are stakes involved here that go beyond ordinary crime. I can't explain everything right now, but I believe it's time we join forces."

Amidst her swirling thoughts and the residual adrenaline, Anjali recognized the genuineness in Rahul's tone. Her journalist instincts, sharpened by years of uncovering concealed narratives, told her that Rahul's involvement was a pivotal piece in the complex puzzle she was unravelling.

"Alright," she consented, her voice embodying the resolve of a seasoned journalist. "But no more secrets. If we're going to do this, complete transparency is non-negotiable." Rahul nodded, an unspoken agreement forged in the dim alleyway. They emerged onto the livelier streets of Bangalore, their steps in unison, marking the beginning of an alliance formed in the crucible of danger and shrouded in enigma.

Over the ensuing days, Anjali and Rahul delved into the labyrinth of cybercrimes that had entangled the city. They spent hours poring over data, drawing connections, and following leads that wove through the digital underbelly of Bangalore. Initially marked by mutual suspicion, their interactions gradually evolved into a partnership cemented by a shared objective.

Anjali found herself increasingly impressed by Rahul's analytical acumen. His ability to decipher patterns and correlations in complex data was exceptional. Conversely, Rahul discovered a newfound respect for Anjali's dogged determination and keen intellect. Despite their divergent backgrounds, they were united in their quest for the truth.

As they collaborated, the initial barriers of mistrust slowly dissolved. Anjali narrated tales of her journalistic escapades, her eyes sparkling with the fervour that fueled her profession. Rahul, though more reticent, opened up about his passion for technology and his commitment to using his expertise for benevolent purposes.

Their investigation led them to a small but significant tech startup named "Quantum Innovations." Recently targeted in a suspicious data breach, the startup was rumoured to be involved in developing advanced encryption technology, potentially used by various clandestine organizations. To infiltrate Quantum Innovations, Anjali and Rahul disguised themselves as consultants. They managed to access the server room, a hub of digital activity where they hoped to find crucial evidence.

Inside the server room, surrounded by the constant hum of machinery and the rhythmic blinking of lights, they sifted through digital data. Their breakthrough came with the discovery of a hidden file, a piece of the puzzle that linked Quantum Innovations to the larger criminal network.

However, their discovery triggered an alarm, forcing them into a hasty retreat. Escaping narrowly, they realized they were up against an adversary always one step ahead.

As they retreated from the building, their hearts racing with the exhilaration and peril of their narrow escape, it dawned on them that they were contending with an adversary who was perpetually a step ahead – a mastermind orchestrating a high-stakes game in the digital arena.

The day's harrowing events solidified their partnership. Anjali and Rahul, the journalist and the analyst, were now bound by a shared mission and the secrets they carried. Together, they embarked on a path fraught with uncertainties and dangers, but turning back was no longer an option. The narrative they were unravelling extended beyond a series of isolated cybercrimes; it was a convoluted plot that meandered through the dark recesses of Bangalore's tech underworld. United by newfound trust and a shared goal, Anjali and Rahul were resolute in their determination to unearth the hidden truths, irrespective of the risks involved.

Ahead of them lay a journey marked by intrigue, peril, and revelations. Their alliance, forged in the alleys of Bangalore and solidified in the face of imminent danger, was the key to exposing a conspiracy that threatened to engulf the city's digital landscape. Together, they ventured deeper into the labyrinth, committed to shedding light on the shadows that lurked within, determined to reveal the story in its entirety to the world.

As the city transitioned from the calm of twilight to the vibrant energy of the night, their partnership, too, evolved from a cautious collaboration to a deep-seated trust and mutual respect. In the days that followed their narrow escape from the tech startup, Anjali and Rahul found themselves delving deeper into a network of deceit that seemed to permeate the city's digital infrastructure. The small, targeted startup was just the tip of the iceberg, a gateway into a labyrinth of cybercrimes that sprawled across Bangalore.

Their investigation took them to various parts of the city, each location providing a unique piece of the complex puzzle they were attempting to solve. They visited rundown buildings that housed hidden server rooms, met with informants in crowded cafes who spoke in hushed tones, and scoured through piles of data in secluded libraries.

As they wove through the city's streets, Anjali's journalistic instincts were in full swing. She was a force of nature, her mind constantly analyzing, connecting dots, and drawing conclusions. Rahul, with his expertise in cybersecurity, complemented her skills perfectly. His technical knowledge and ability to decipher complex data patterns were invaluable in navigating the digital maze they were exploring. Their partnership was not without challenges. Long hours, constant vigilance, and the ever-present danger lurking in the shadows took their toll. There were moments of doubt and fear, times when the magnitude of what they were up against seemed overwhelming. But in these moments, their newfound alliance provided strength and support.

One evening, as they sat in a small café going over their latest findings, Rahul looked up from his laptop, his expression serious. "Anjali, we're getting closer to the heart of this network. But the deeper we go, the more dangerous it becomes. Are you sure you're ready for what might come next?" Anjali met his gaze, her determination unwavering. "I've been chasing stories all my life, Rahul. But this... this is more than just a story. It's about exposing the truth, no matter how perilous the path. I'm ready."

Rahul nodded, a look of admiration in his eyes. "Then let's see this through to the end, together."

Their investigation led them to uncover a series of interconnected crimes – financial fraud, data theft, and illegal surveillance operations. It became clear that the network they were uncovering was not just a group of rogue hackers but a well-organized syndicate with far-reaching influence.

As they unravelled the layers of the conspiracy, they also uncovered evidence of corruption within the ranks of those who were supposed to protect the city. It was a shocking revelation that added a new level of complexity to their investigation. Determined to bring the truth to light, Anjali and Rahul planned their next move. They compiled their evidence, meticulously documenting every detail of the network's operations. But they knew that exposing the syndicate would not be easy. They needed a strategy that would protect them from the inevitable backlash.

The night before they were set to meet with a trusted official in the police department, Anjali and Rahul met in a quiet park, the city lights twinkling in the distance. The weight of what they were about to do hung heavily in the air. "Once we hand over this evidence, there's no turning back," Rahul said, his voice low. "We'll be exposing not just the criminals but also those who have been aiding them. It's going to shake the city to its core."

Anjali looked at him, her resolve clear in her eyes. "That's a risk we have to take. This city, and its people, deserve to know the truth. And we're the only ones who can bring it to them."

Their meeting with the police official the next day was a turning point. The evidence they presented was irrefutable, setting off a chain of events that would rock the city. Raids were conducted, arrests were made, and the story of the syndicate's takedown made headlines.

But the journey was far from over. As the dust settled, Anjali and Rahul knew that their alliance had changed them. They had started as strangers, brought together by circumstance, but had emerged as partners in a crusade for justice. In the aftermath of the syndicate's exposure, they continued to work together, their partnership evolving into a deep, unspoken bond. They had faced danger, uncovered dark truths, and emerged victorious. But more importantly, they had found in each other an ally, a confidante, and a friend.

The city of Bangalore, with its ever-changing landscape and hidden secrets, had been the backdrop of their incredible journey. As they walked through its streets, now familiar with the secrets they had uncovered, Anjali and Rahul knew that their alliance was a testament to the power of collaboration and the unyielding pursuit of truth. Under the canopy of a starlit sky, they stood together, looking out at the city that had been the stage of their remarkable journey. They had come a long way from the dim alleyway where their alliance was formed. And as they looked ahead, they knew that there were more stories to uncover, more truths to bring to light. But whatever the future held, they were ready to face it, together.

Chasing Shadows

The new day in Bangalore brought the first light of dawn and a renewed sense of purpose for Anjali and Rahul. As the city awoke, bathed in soft pinks and oranges, the familiar cacophony of urban life resumed. It was amidst this daily resurgence that Anjali and Rahul found themselves at the heart of the city's sprawling tech hub, a place pulsating with the energy of innovation, ambition, and a relentless drive towards progress.

This particular morning felt different for Anjali. The tech hub, usually a canvas for her journalistic endeavours, now represented a deeper involvement. She was no longer just a bystander documenting the stories of technological triumphs and tribulations. Instead, she was an integral part of a narrative that delved into the more concealed aspects of this glittering world. Her emotions were a blend of anticipation, determination, and a hint of apprehension about what lay ahead.

Rahul, accustomed to the rhythms and nuances of the tech environment, navigated through the crowd with focused intent. His eyes were alert, always observing, reflecting his deep connection to and understanding of the tech world. His background in cybersecurity has given him a unique perspective on the tech hub, allowing him to see beyond the surface-level innovations and into the complexities that lay beneath.

As they walked, their steps in sync, there was a shared understanding between them. They were partners in a mission much larger than themselves, a mission that involved unravelling the intricacies of a sprawling digital conspiracy. Their journey had brought them to this place, where the boundaries between technological advancements and the darker side of progress blurred.

Their destination stood out amidst the cityscape – a building that exuded modernity and sophistication, its sleek, contemporary architecture a stark contrast to the traditional buildings that dotted other parts of Bangalore. This structure housed a startup that had recently become the target of a sophisticated cyberattack – an incident that had sent shockwaves through the tech community.

Upon entering, they were immediately engulfed in the characteristic energy of a startup. The open-plan workspace buzzed with activity – young professionals engrossed in their screens, engaging in animated discussions, or lost in deep concentration. The air was charged with a palpable sense of urgency and drive, typical of a company fueled by innovation and youthful zeal. They were ushered into a compact conference room, where they were greeted by Ayesha Khan, the CEO. In her late twenties, Ayesha exuded a blend of professional sharpness and the informal vibe of startup culture. However, it was the intensity in her eyes that captured Anjali's attention – a fierce determination mingled with a hint of recent anxiety, indicating that the cyberattack had left more than just operational disruptions in its wake.

Rahul initiated the conversation, his questions laser-focused and incisive, cutting through the complexities of the cybersecurity breach. Anjali observed Ayesha intently, noting the minute changes in her expression, and the occasional faltering in her voice. The attack had clearly left a profound impact, shaking the foundations of Ayesha's confidence in her enterprise.

As Rahul probed deeper into the specifics of the attack, Anjali's journalistic instincts were in overdrive. The pieces of information they gathered began forming a mosaic that was both intriguing and disconcerting. This cyberattack on Ayesha's startup was not a random act of digital vandalism; it was a meticulously planned operation, a cog in a larger, more ominous plot.

Following the meeting, Anjali and Rahul retreated to a nearby café, a cosy establishment that offered respite from the hubbub of the tech world. The café, with its aroma of freshly brewed coffee and a quiet ambience, provided the perfect backdrop for their debriefing. Seated in a secluded corner, away from the soft murmurs of other patrons, Anjali felt a sense of camaraderie with Rahul, a connection forged through shared goals and experiences. Yet, she sensed an unspoken barrier, an invisible wall Rahul had erected around his personal life.

Over steaming cups of coffee, they pieced together their findings. Rahul's insights were razor-sharp, each observation a testament to his profound understanding of the digital landscape. Anjali, with her innate journalistic flair, connected his technical explanations into a coherent narrative that began to shed light on the perplexing web they were unravelling.

Yet, as they conversed, Anjali couldn't shake off the feeling that Rahul was holding back, that behind his composed exterior lay secrets integral to the mystery they were chasing. She mentally noted to probe further, to peel back not just the layers of the story at hand, but also the layers of Rahul's guarded persona.

Leaving the café, they stepped back into the dynamic environment of the tech hub. Anjali realized that their investigation was leading them down a path fraught with unknowns and potential perils. But one thing was clear – she and Rahul were now inextricably linked in this journey, partners in a quest that blurred the lines between shadows and truths.

In the days that followed, Anjali and Rahul delved deeper into the heart of the conspiracy. They tracked down leads, analyzed patterns, and interrogated sources, each step uncovering more of the elusive truth. Their partnership was a delicate balance of trust and caution, as they navigated a maze of deception and half-truths.

Anjali's reporting skills complemented Rahul's technical expertise, allowing them to uncover layers of the conspiracy that had remained hidden. Rahul, in turn, was constantly amazed by Anjali's tenacity and her ability to discern truth from fiction. Together, they were more than just a journalist and a cybersecurity analyst; they were a formidable team, united in their quest for truth.

Their investigation took them to various corners of the city, from high-tech offices to dingy internet cafes, each location providing a piece of the intricate puzzle they were assembling. They encountered a myriad of characters – from ambitious tech entrepreneurs to disillusioned former employees, each adding a layer to the complex narrative they were uncovering.

As they unravelled the web of deceit and corruption, Anjali and Rahul found themselves confronting not just digital criminals but a network that extended into the realms of power and influence. Their investigation brought them face-to-face with the harsh realities of ambition, greed, and the lengths people would go to protect their interests. Despite the obstacles and dangers, Anjali and Rahul pressed on, their determination fueled by the knowledge that they were on the brink of a significant discovery. They knew that the story they were unravelling had the potential to shake the foundations of Bangalore's tech industry, to bring to light the hidden machinations that operated in the shadows.

Through late-night discussions, endless analysis, and relentless pursuit, Anjali and Rahul pieced together the final pieces of the puzzle. They uncovered a conspiracy that was vast and complex, a network of cybercriminals intricately linked to some of the city's most influential figures.

As they stood on the precipice of exposing the truth, Anjali and Rahul realized that their journey had changed them. They were no longer just individuals driven by their respective professions; they had become allies in a fight against a hidden enemy, partners in a battle to bring truth to light. The dawn in Bangalore heralded not just a new day but a new phase in Anjali and Rahul's investigation. They had delved deep into the labyrinth of cybercrimes, navigating a world where the lines between right and wrong, legal and illegal, were often blurred. Now, as the city woke up to the hustle of daily life, they found themselves on the brink of a major breakthrough, one that could potentially shake the very foundations of Bangalore's tech industry.

Amidst the pulsating energy of innovation and ambition, Anjali and Rahul continued their quest. The information they had gathered from Ayesha's startup had opened up a Pandora's box, revealing a network far more intricate and widespread than they had initially anticipated. Their journey took them to the darker corners of the city, where the sheen of technological advancement gave way to the grim reality of exploitation and corruption. They met with whistleblowers in dingy, anonymous coffee shops, exchanged covert messages with insiders, and sifted through reams of data in search of the elusive threads that would tie the entire narrative together.

Each discovery they made added to the complexity of the case. The network they were up against was not just a group of opportunistic hackers; it was a well-organized syndicate with deep connections in the tech world and beyond. The implications of their findings were enormous, and with each step forward, the danger to themselves became increasingly apparent. One evening, as they reviewed their findings in the safety of Anjali's apartment, Rahul looked up from his laptop, his expression grave. "Anjali, the deeper we go, the more I realize the scale of what we're up against. This isn't just about cybercrime; it's about power, control, and a level of manipulation that's chilling."

Anjali nodded, her eyes reflecting the seriousness of the situation. "I know, Rahul. But we can't back down now. This story... it's bigger than both of us. We owe it to the city to expose this corruption." Their dedication to the cause saw them working tirelessly, often at the expense of their personal lives. The more they uncovered, the more they realized the extent of the syndicate's reach. It wasn't just individuals or corporations that were involved; there were hints of involvement at higher levels of power, implicating figures in positions of authority.

Despite the risks, they pressed on, driven by a sense of duty and a desire for justice. They knew that they were the city's best hope for uncovering the truth behind the facade of technological advancement. Their investigation led them to a critical lead - a series of encrypted emails that hinted at a meeting between key players in the syndicate. The meeting was to take place at an upscale hotel in the city, a location that offered both privacy and luxury. Knowing the risks, Anjali and Rahul decided to infiltrate the meeting. Disguised and equipped with hidden recording devices, they entered the world of the elite, where deals were made over expensive drinks and handshakes.

The meeting was a revelation. The key players were there, discussing plans with a casual arrogance that spoke of their untouchable status. Anjali and Rahul recorded everything, aware that what they were capturing could be the key to bringing down the entire network. After the meeting, as they made their way out of the hotel, the weight of their discovery hung heavy between them. They had in their possession evidence that could change the course of their investigation, evidence that was both powerful and dangerous.

Back in their makeshift headquarters, they reviewed the recordings, piecing together the final parts of the puzzle. The network was planning a major operation, one that would have far-reaching consequences for the city and its inhabitants. Knowing the urgency of the situation, Anjali and Rahul worked through the night, preparing a report that would blow the lid off the syndicate's operations. They planned to release the information to the public, exposing the network's activities and its connections to influential figures.

The following day, as the report went live, the city was rocked by the revelations. The media picked up the story immediately, broadcasting the details of the syndicate's operations and the involvement of high-profile individuals. The impact was immediate and far-reaching. Law enforcement agencies launched investigations, arrests were made, and the tech community was forced to confront the dark side of its meteoric rise.

For Anjali and Rahul, the release of the report marked the culmination of months of hard work and danger. They had exposed one of the city's biggest criminal networks, but in doing so, they had also made powerful enemies. In the aftermath of the revelations, they knew that their lives would never be the same. They had started as strangers, brought together by a shared goal, but had emerged as partners in a fight against corruption and injustice.

As they sat together, watching the city react to their discoveries, they realized that their journey wasn't over yet. They had chased shadows and uncovered truths that many would have preferred remained hidden. But now, more than ever, they knew they needed to stay vigilant, to continue their fight for justice. As they looked out over the city, they knew that their alliance had changed them, forged in the crucible of their shared experiences.

As the sun set over Bangalore, casting a golden hue over the city they had fought to protect, Anjali and Rahul knew that their alliance, born of necessity, had evolved into something much more profound – a partnership that would endure through whatever challenges the future might hold.

Unseen Connections

After their profound discoveries, Anjali and Rahul embarked on a new phase of their investigation. The early light of dawn in Bangalore not only heralded a new day but also signified a deeper plunge into the city's past. This transition from the high-tech world to the historical heart of Bangalore marked a pivotal shift in their journey. Their path led them through the labyrinthine lanes of the city's old quarters, a stark contrast to the sleek, digital landscapes they had been navigating. Here, amidst the echoes of a storied past, every street corner and aged building whispered tales of bygone eras, providing a rich tapestry of history for their investigation.

As they meandered past bustling bazaars, where the vibrant energy of commerce and life was palpable, they encountered the enduring legacy of ancient temples and colonial architecture. These structures stood as silent witnesses to the city's evolution, their façades etched with stories from a time long past.

Their search brought them to an old library, a repository of knowledge that seemed untouched by the relentless march of time. The library, nestled among more modern edifices, held a mystique that drew them in. Its ornate façade and the scent of aged books created an atmosphere of reverence, a stark departure from the dynamic pulse of the tech hub they were accustomed to.

Greeted by the librarian, whose presence seemed as age-old as the books he tended, Anjali and Rahul found themselves delving into the past to uncover connections to their present investigation. "We're tracing the roots of digital crimes, particularly from about a decade ago," Anjali explained, her voice a mix of curiosity and determination. The librarian, with a knowing nod, guided them through the archives. His words, "Ah, the digital age has its own shadows, some that stretch far into the corners of our past," resonated with the duo, highlighting the intersection of the historical and the digital in their quest.

Surrounded by the tranquillity of the library, their investigation took on a sacred quality. They sifted through old newspapers and manuscripts, uncovering layers of history that paralleled their current case. It was in this solemn setting that Anjali stumbled upon a startling piece of information - an article that detailed the exploits of a notorious hacker group. One name, in particular, stood out - 'Arjun Mehra.'

Rahul's reaction to the mention of this name was immediate and visceral. His usually composed demeanour faltered, revealing a connection to his past that Anjali had not seen before. Her probing question, "Rahul, what aren't you telling me?" broke the silence, underscoring the growing trust and partnership between them.

Rahul's admission of his past, his association with Arjun, and his departure from a life that had set him on a destructive path were revelations that deepened their connection. This newfound understanding between them was a significant turning point in their journey, transforming their professional alliance into a personal bond. As they stepped out of the library, the world of old Bangalore enveloped them. The city's historic charm and the hustle of daily life contrasted sharply with the quiet introspection they had just experienced. Anjali's insistence on understanding the full picture of Rahul's past, and his subsequent openness, marked a new level of trust in their relationship.

Their walk through the city that evening was reflective, a time to process the revelations of the day. Rahul's confession about his past and his fears of how it might change Anjali's perception of him highlighted the depth of their bond. Anjali's supportive response, and her assurance that they were facing these challenges together, solidified their partnership.

As night fell, Anjali and Rahul recognized that their investigation had evolved into something much more profound. No longer just a pursuit of digital criminals, it had become a journey of personal discovery, of confronting past demons and forging new paths. Their conversation, delving into the implications of Rahul's past and its connections to their current case, was a testament to their combined strengths. Anjali's journalistic insight and Rahul's technical expertise were now complemented by a mutual understanding and shared experiences.

The night in Bangalore, with its blend of history and modernity, mirrored their journey - a path that had taken them from the digital frontiers of the tech hub to the historical depths of the city's heart. It was a journey that had revealed the unseen connections between the past and the present, between individual stories and the larger narrative they were uncovering. As they parted ways, promising to continue their work the next day, they knew that the dawn of a new day would bring new challenges and new revelations, but they were ready to face them together. Their alliance, forged in the pursuit of truth and strengthened by shared vulnerabilities, had become a powerful force, ready to illuminate the unseen connections and bring to light the hidden truths of Bangalore's digital landscape.

Anjali and Rahul found themselves at a significant juncture in their investigation. The echoes of Rahul's past revelations still lingered, intertwining with the maze of digital deceit they were unravelling. The historical heart of the city, with its whispered tales and aged wisdom, had opened a new vista in their quest, merging the past with the present. Their day began with a return to the labyrinthine alleys of old Bangalore, where the city's heritage stood in stark contrast to the tech hub's modernity. The ancient temples and colonial architecture were not just silent witnesses to history but custodians of secrets that now seemed more relevant than ever.

As they navigated through the bustling bazaars, Anjali's mind was a whirlwind of thoughts, piecing together the fragments of information they had gathered. Beside her, Rahul walked with a sense of determination, the revelations of his past now a driving force in their pursuit of truth.

Their next stop was an archival centre, a place where the city's history was meticulously preserved. Here, amid rows of old documents and fading photographs, they hoped to find clues that would link the city's storied past to the cybercrimes of the present.

The archivist, a woman of middle age with an air of scholarly wisdom, greeted them with a knowing look. "I heard about your investigation. You're treading on uncharted territory," she said, leading them to a section of the archives that held records of the city's technological evolution. Pouring over old blueprints and documents, Anjali and Rahul discovered a pattern - a series of discreet communications and transactions that dated back decades, suggesting that the roots of the cybercrime syndicate were deeper and more entangled in the city's fabric than they had anticipated.

Their research was interrupted by an urgent message from one of Rahul's contacts. A breakthrough had occurred - a whistleblower from within the syndicate had come forward, willing to share information. The meeting was set in a discreet location, away from the prying eyes of the city. Under the cover of dusk, Anjali and Rahul met with the informant, a shadowy figure cloaked in anonymity. The informant's revelations were explosive - the syndicate was planning a massive cyberattack on the city's infrastructure, one that could cripple Bangalore's technological backbone.

The gravity of the situation weighed heavily on them. They now held information that could prevent a disaster, but the clock was ticking. The syndicate was aware of the breach and was moving quickly to cover its tracks. With newfound urgency, Anjali and Rahul strategized their next move. They needed to act fast, to bring this information to the authorities and avert the impending crisis. The night was spent in a flurry of activity, consolidating evidence and formulating a plan.

As dawn broke over the city, marking the beginning of a crucial day, they met with a trusted law enforcement official. The evidence they presented was compelling, leading to an immediate mobilization of resources to counter the threatened cyberattack. The following hours were tense, with Anjali, Rahul, and a team of cybersecurity experts and law enforcement officers monitoring the situation from a secure command centre. Unbeknownst to the city's millions of inhabitants, it was on the brink of a technological catastrophe.

The climax came as the syndicate initiated its attack, launching a sophisticated onslaught on the city's digital infrastructure. Thanks to the information provided by Anjali and Rahul, the authorities were prepared, and the attack was thwarted, the syndicate's plans foiled. In the aftermath of the crisis, Anjali and Rahul were hailed as heroes, their efforts having saved the city from an unprecedented disaster. However, their journey was far from over. The syndicate, though weakened, remained at large, with its key members shrouded in the shadows.

The days that followed were a mix of debriefings, interviews, and strategizing for the next steps. The story of their success spread across the city, bringing them acclaim as well as a renewed sense of danger. The syndicate would likely retaliate, and they needed to be prepared. Amidst the chaos, Anjali and Rahul found solace in each other's company. Their bond had been forged through adversity and shared experiences, evolving beyond the confines of professional collaboration. They were a united team, driven by their quest for truth and justice.

Continuing their investigation, they delved deeper into the syndicate's operations, encountering new challenges. The web of deceit was complex, spanning different sectors and involving influential figures. Their pursuit led them to uncover hidden agendas, corrupt alliances, and a network that operated in the shadows. The scale of the conspiracy was daunting, but Anjali and Rahul were undeterred, driven by a relentless pursuit of truth and a desire to bring the perpetrators to justice.

Their journey took them to the far reaches of the city, to places where the glossy facade of the tech hub gave way to the grim realities of power and greed. They met with sources in clandestine locations, pieced together evidence from covert operations, and faced threats that tested their resolve.

Throughout their journey, Anjali's journalistic instincts and Rahul's technical expertise were their guiding lights. They navigated through a maze of misinformation and danger, with their partnership serving as a beacon of hope in the quest for justice.

From the tech hub's high-rise buildings to the old city's narrow lanes, they traced the unseen connections that tied the city's past to its present, its digital frontiers to its hidden underworld. As they delved deeper into the heart of the syndicate, uncovering layer after layer of deception, Anjali and Rahul knew that their journey was far from over. They had become more than just investigators; they were guardians of the truth, champions of justice in a city that was a microcosm of the digital age.

Their story, born amidst the chaos of a bustling tech hub and nurtured through trials and triumphs, was a testament to the resilience of the human spirit. It was a story of courage and determination, of unseen connections and unbreakable bonds. The night in Bangalore, with its canopy of stars and the quiet hum of the city, bore witness to their journey - a journey that had taken them from the realms of digital crimes to the depths of human greed, from the shadows of the past to the light of the present.

As they stood together, looking out over the city that had been the stage for their remarkable journey, Anjali and Rahul knew that their story was far from over. The challenges ahead were many, but they were ready to face them, united in their mission, and steadfast in their pursuit of justice. As the city slept, their alliance stood strong - a partnership forged in adversity, a union that had transcended the boundaries of their professions. Together, they were a force to be reckoned with, ready to chase down the shadows and unveil the unseen connections that lay hidden in the city's digital landscape.

Their journey was a journey of discovery, a pursuit of truth in a world where the lines between right and wrong were often blurred. And as the first light of dawn began to break over the horizon, signalling the start of a new day, Anjali and Rahul set out once again, their determination unwavering, their resolve unbreakable. Their story continued - a story of chasing shadows, of uncovering unseen connections, a story that was as much about their personal transformation as it was about their quest for justice. And as they walked through the streets, their steps in harmony, they knew that their journey was a testament to the power of unity, the strength of partnership, and the enduring quest for truth in a city that was a microcosm of the modern world.

Tangled Webs

The investigation into the city's web of cybercrimes had become the epicentre of Rahul and Anjali's lives. Nights blurred into mornings in a relentless pursuit of elusive truths, their existence oscillating between the tangible reality of Bangalore's bustling streets and the shadowy realm of digital deception. With each passing day, they delved deeper into a labyrinth that seemed to sprawl endlessly beneath the city's vibrant facade.

One moonless night, acting on a tip about a crucial lead, they found themselves navigating the serpentine alleys of an older part of Bangalore. The narrow passage, flanked by ancient buildings standing like silent witnesses to countless untold stories, exuded an air of mystery. The tip, a sliver of hope in their complex investigation, promised a step closer to untangling the intricate network of digital crimes that had enshrouded the city.

But as they ventured deeper, an unsettling sense of being watched crept over them. Suddenly, figures emerged from the shadows, materializing like phantoms. There was no time to think, only a split-second to react. Adrenaline surged as Rahul and Anjali found themselves thrust into a physical confrontation. Their attackers, swift and silent, moved with deadly precision. Anjali, usually driven by her journalistic instincts, now found herself propelled by a primal urge to survive and protect. Beside her, Rahul, his past a hidden chapter, displayed surprising proficiency in defence, his movements a silent testament to skills honed in a life he had left behind.

The clash was a tempest of motion in the alley's confines, a desperate struggle for survival. Anjali and Rahul fought with a synergy born of their shared experiences, their movements synchronized in a dance of survival. And when the skirmish ended, as abruptly as it had begun, with their assailants disappearing back into the night, they were left in the aftermath, shaken but unharmed.

Leaning against the cold, rough walls of the alley, they caught their breath, the silence around them a stark contrast to the chaos that had just ensued. Rahul looked at Anjali, his expression a mixture of concern and newfound respect. "You're quite the fighter," he said, a hint of a smile touching his lips.

Anjali, still coming to terms with the night's events, returned a wry smile. "Looks like we make a pretty good team," she responded, her voice betraying a hint of surprise at their unexpected combativeness.

In that charged moment, amidst the danger and uncertainty, their bond solidified. It was more than professional now; it was a mutual reliance and respect that transcended the boundaries of their initial partnership.

As they stepped back onto the city's better-lit streets, the urban landscape seemed to have transformed. The city lights flickered like distant stars, casting a surreal glow over the streets. The danger they had just faced was a visceral reminder of the high stakes of their investigation, of the unseen threats lurking in the city's shadows.

Yet, the fear that once overshadowed their journey had morphed into a driving force, fueling their determination. No longer were they just a journalist and cybersecurity experts; they were allies in a perilous dance with danger, unravelling a narrative that intertwined their destinies with the city's concealed darkness.

Their investigation was far from concluded. The mystery continued to weave its intricate web, each clue they uncovered bringing them a step closer to the heart of the enigma. But one thing was crystal clear – Rahul and Anjali were in this together, and their partnership was strengthened by each challenge they faced.

As they navigated the city's labyrinthine streets, their conversation turned to the events of the night. "I never expected our investigation to take such a turn," Anjali remarked her tone a mix of reflection and resolve.

Rahul nodded in agreement. "Neither did I. But it's clear now that we're dealing with something much bigger than we initially thought. There are forces at play here that don't want us to uncover the truth."

Anjali's eyes held a determined glint. "Then we must be doing something right. We're getting closer, Rahul. I can feel it."

Their path led them through the city's diverse tapestry – from bustling marketplaces alive with the night's commerce to quiet residential areas where the city's heartbeat slowed to a gentle rhythm. With each step, they wove their story into the city's complex narrative.

The night's events had opened a new chapter in their investigation, one where danger was a tangible presence, lurking just out of sight. But it had also deepened their connection, forging a partnership that was resilient and dynamic.

As they parted ways for the night, silently pledging to continue their pursuit the next day, they each carried the weight of the night's revelations and an unspoken acknowledgement of their deepening bond. In the solitude of her apartment, Anjali reflected on the journey thus far. The investigation had begun as a professional endeavour but had evolved into a personal crusade, drawing her closer to Rahul in unexpected ways. His revelations, his skills, and their shared experiences had woven a complex tapestry of trust and reliance.

Meanwhile, Rahul grappled with the duality of his past and present. The night's encounter had resurrected memories he had long tried to bury, yet it had also revealed a strength in Anjali that he admired and resonated with. Their partnership, born out of necessity, had grown into a bond that was both challenging and rewarding.

As dawn broke, casting the first light on a city that never truly slept, Rahul and Anjali prepared to continue their journey. The mystery they unravelled was not merely a series of digital footprints and hidden crimes; it was a story of resilience, courage, and an unwavering pursuit of truth. In the heart of the city, as the new day began, they stood ready to confront whatever challenges lay ahead. Together, they would navigate the tangled webs of their investigation, each step drawing them closer to the elusive truth and a deeper understanding of their own connection.

With the first light of daybreak filtering through the bustling city, Rahul and Anjali set out once more, their steps resonating with determination on the streets of Bangalore. The previous night's encounter had left an indelible mark on their journey, forging a bond grounded in mutual trust and an unspoken understanding.

Their next lead directed them to a seemingly inconspicuous café in a busy part of the city, rumoured to be a covert meeting spot for individuals involved in the cybercrime network. The café, with its unremarkable exterior, contrasted sharply with the world of high-tech crimes they were delving into.

Inside, amidst the clatter of cups and the murmur of conversations, they discreetly occupied a corner table. Anjali's keen eyes scanned the room, taking note of the patrons, while Rahul remained vigilant, alert to any sign of the contact they were supposed to meet.

"Do you think our contact will show up?" Anjali whispered, her gaze still surveying the café.

Rahul nodded subtly, his eyes never leaving the entrance. "If our information is correct, they should. This place is more than it appears."

Their wait was interrupted by the arrival of a figure who seemed out of place in the casual café setting. The man, dressed inconspicuously, approached their table. His sharp, calculating eyes briefly met theirs before he took his seat.

"Rahul, Anjali," he greeted in a low tone, his voice barely audible over the café's hum. "I'm glad you decided to meet. What you're chasing is bigger than you realize."

Anjali leaned forward, her journalistic instincts piqued. "What can you tell us? We need information that can lead us to the core of this network."

The man glanced around cautiously before responding. "The network you're trying to uncover, it's not just a group of rogue hackers. It's a syndicate with deep roots and connections that reach far beyond Bangalore."

Rahul's expression hardened. "Do you have names? Evidence?"

The man slid a USB drive across the table. "Everything you need is here. But be careful. The people involved are dangerous, and they won't hesitate to silence anyone who gets too close."

As swiftly as he had appeared, the man stood up and departed, blending into the crowd. Rahul and Anjali exchanged a knowing look, the weight of responsibility now squarely upon their shoulders.

Exiting the café with the USB securely tucked away, they understood that their investigation had reached a pivotal juncture. The information they had just received could be the key to unravelling the network, but it also marked them as targets for those they sought to expose.

The day was spent in a secluded location, where they meticulously combed through the data from the USB drive. It was a treasure trove of information – names, transactions, covert communications – painting a picture of a criminal network more intricate and far-reaching than they had initially imagined.

"This goes beyond cybercrime," Anjali remarked, her voice tinged with a mix of awe and apprehension. "It's a web of corruption, blackmail, and illegal activities."

Rahul, who had been engrossed in analysis, looked up. "And at the centre of it all is a name that keeps reappearing. It's like a shadow orchestrating the entire operation." The gravity of their discovery hung heavily in the room. They were teetering on the precipice of exposing a criminal empire, but the path forward was fraught with danger.

As evening descended upon Bangalore, Rahul and Anjali found themselves at a crossroads. The information they had unearthed was crucial, but it also placed them in jeopardy. They needed a plan, a strategy to disseminate the information without falling victim to the very criminals they were exposing.

"We need to be strategic about this," Rahul suggested, his mind racing with possibilities. "We can't simply hand this over to the authorities, not until we can trust them completely."

Anjali concurred with a nod. "We must find a way to make this information public, to ensure our safety, and to bring down the network." The decision was made, and they set about crafting a plan to leak the information to the media and trusted contacts within law enforcement. It was a perilous move, but it was the only card they had to play.

In the subsequent days, their plan was put into action. The data from the USB drive was encrypted and shared with various news outlets and trusted contacts, laying bare the syndicate's activities and exposing the individuals involved.

The repercussions were immediate and explosive. News reports dominated the headlines, law enforcement agencies were galvanized into action, and the city buzzed with the revelation of the criminal network that had thrived beneath its surface.

However, for Rahul and Anjali, the battle was far from over. They understood that exposing the network was only the initial step. There were still individuals who would attempt to silence them, and the shadow at the heart of the web remained elusive. Their journey together had led them into the heart of the darkness lurking beneath the city's vibrant exterior. Yet, as they stood side by side, united in their purpose and their burgeoning bond, they found solace in knowing they had each other's backs.

Bangalore, with its myriad lights and shadows, mirrored their journey – a blend of danger, intrigue, and an unwavering quest for truth. Amidst it all, Rahul and Anjali had stumbled upon something unexpected – a partnership as profound as it was perilous. As they braced for the next phase of their journey, with the cityscape stretching before them, they were keenly aware that the path ahead would be fraught with challenges. But armed with their combined skills, unwavering determination, and the trust they had forged, they were resolute in their readiness to confront whatever lay ahead.

The air was pregnant with the anticipation of what the next phase of their investigation would unveil, and the streets seemed like a labyrinth of light and shadow that mirrored the intricacies of the web they were untangling. The discovery at the café, the USB drive laden with incriminating evidence, had propelled their investigation into uncharted territory. Now, as they ventured through the quieter corners of the city, their minds buzzed with strategies and the weight of responsibility.

"We're on the cusp of something monumental," Anjali whispered, her voice barely audible above the city's hum. "This evidence has the potential to dismantle the entire network."

Rahul nodded, his gaze fixed on the path ahead. "But it's not just about exposing them. We must ensure our safety too. We've witnessed how far they're willing to go." Their conversation wove planning and reflection into a delicate dance of words, intertwining their fears with their professional resolve. As they walked, they discussed the implications of their findings, the potential fallout, and the cautious steps they needed to take to dismantle the syndicate without jeopardizing their safety.

As dawn approached, painting the sky in shades of amber and gold, they stood before an old, abandoned building that had once been a hub of technological innovation. Now, it stood as a relic of the past, a symbol of the city's rapid evolution.

"This place," Rahul mused, gazing up at the building, "it's a reminder of how quickly things change, of how the past can be swallowed up by the present." Anjali nodded, her eyes reflecting the building's eerie silhouette. "And yet, the past has a way of creeping back, of making itself known when we least expect it." Their investigation had taught them that the city's history was deeply intertwined with its present and that the roots of the cybercrimes they were investigating stretched back further than they had initially thought. The abandoned building was a physical manifestation of that realization.

As they entered the building, their footsteps echoed in the empty halls, a haunting reminder of the fragility of progress. They were acutely aware of how easily the advancements of today could become the forgotten relics of tomorrow.

Their search through the building was meticulous, each room was scoured for any hint of a connection to the syndicate. It was here, in the heart of forgotten innovation, that they stumbled upon a crucial piece of evidence – a set of encrypted files that had been left behind, overlooked in the building's hasty abandonment.

The files were a treasure trove of information, providing deeper insights into the syndicate's operations and connections. Names, dates, and plans were laid out in a digital trail that painted a picture of corruption and manipulation spanning decades. "We've got them," Anjali exclaimed, her voice tinged with a mix of triumph and disbelief. "This is it, Rahul. This is the evidence we need to bring them down."

But even as they celebrated their discovery, the weight of what lay ahead was not lost on them. The syndicate would not go down without a fight, and the evidence they now held made them prime targets.

Their return to the heart of the city was marked by a sense of urgency. They knew they had to act swiftly, to get the evidence into the right hands before the syndicate could mobilize against them. The city's streets were now bathed in the light of dawn, the early morning sun casting long shadows that seemed to follow Anjali and Rahul as they made their way to their next meeting – a rendezvous with a trusted ally in the police force.

The meeting, held in a nondescript coffee shop, was tense. The police officer, a grizzled veteran with years of experience, listened intently as Anjali and Rahul laid out their findings. "This is explosive," the officer remarked, his eyes scanning the documents. "With this evidence, we can take down the entire network. But you two need to be careful. You've just painted a target on your backs."

Anjali and Rahul nodded, their resolve undiminished. "We knew the risks when we started this," Anjali said. "We can't back down now. Not when we're this close." The officer promised to mobilize a task force and take swift action based on the evidence. As Anjali and Rahul left the coffee shop, there was a sense of accomplishment, of a job well done, but also a palpable sense of danger.

The days that followed were a whirlwind of activity. Raids were conducted, arrests were made, and the syndicate's network began to crumble under the weight of the evidence. The city was abuzz with the news, the media frenzy feeding off each new development. But for Anjali and Rahul, the victory was bittersweet. They had exposed the syndicate, but in doing so, they had exposed themselves to unknown dangers. They were now figures of public interest, their faces recognized, their movements watched. Their days were no longer their own, consumed by meetings, interviews, and constant vigilance. The once-clear line between their professional and personal lives had blurred, their investigation now an integral part of who they were.

As they navigated through this new reality, their partnership became their anchor. They relied on each other for support, strength, and the courage to face each new challenge.

One evening, as they sat in Anjali's apartment, reviewing the day's events, Rahul looked at her with a sense of gratitude in his eyes. "I couldn't have done this without you, Anjali. You've been more than a partner in this. You've been a friend, a confidant." Anjali smiled, reaching out to squeeze his hand. "We did this together, Rahul. We faced the darkness and emerged into the light. We're a team in every sense of the word."

Their journey had transformed them, bringing them closer in ways they could never have anticipated. They had started as two individuals, united by a shared mission, but had emerged as partners, bound by a deep and unbreakable bond. The syndicate had been dismantled, but the city still held secrets, stories that needed to be uncovered.

As they prepared to face whatever lay ahead, they knew they were ready. Together, they had navigated the tangled webs of deception and emerged stronger, wiser, and more united than ever before. Anjali and Rahul stood poised to confront the challenges that lay ahead. Their alliance was a beacon of hope in a city that mirrored the modern world. They were prepared to continue, to chase down the shadows and unearth the truths that remained concealed in the city's digital landscape.

In the days that followed, the city of Bangalore buzzed with the aftermath of the exposé. The media's coverage was relentless, with news outlets dissecting every detail of the syndicate's downfall. It was a triumph for justice, a victory over the forces of darkness that had lurked beneath the city's surface for so long. But amidst the celebrations and the sense of accomplishment, Anjali and Rahul remained vigilant. They knew that the syndicate's reach extended beyond the city limits, and there were still loose ends to tie up.

Their days were a whirlwind of interviews and debriefings. Law enforcement agencies from across the country were eager to learn from their findings, and their evidence had become the linchpin in dismantling similar networks in other cities. As they sat in a conference room, surrounded by officials and investigators, Anjali couldn't help but feel a sense of pride. "We did it," she whispered to Rahul. "We made a difference."

Rahul nodded, his expression a mix of satisfaction and weariness. "But we're not done yet. There are still unanswered questions, and I have a feeling the syndicate won't just fade away." Anjali understood his concerns. The shadowy figure at the centre of the web had remained elusive, and some key players had managed to elude the authorities' grasp. Their investigation was far from over.

One evening, as they sat in Anjali's apartment, their laptops open and their notes scattered around them, Rahul looked at her with a serious expression. "Anjali, we need to find out who's behind all of this. We can't rest until we expose the puppeteer pulling the strings." Anjali nodded in agreement. "I've been thinking the same thing. We can't let this person continue to operate in the shadows." Their decision was clear – they needed to dig deeper, to follow the trail of breadcrumbs that would lead them to the syndicate's mastermind. It was a risky endeavour, but they were not ones to back down from a challenge.

Their investigation took them to the darkest corners of the internet, where encrypted messages and hidden forums held the key to the syndicate's operations. They worked tirelessly, their partnership stronger than ever, as they unravelled the digital threads that connected the criminals. One night, as they delved deeper into the digital labyrinth, Rahul suddenly froze. His eyes were fixed on the screen, his fingers flying across the keyboard. "Anjali, I've found something," he said, his voice tinged with excitement. Anjali leaned in to see what had caught his attention. On the screen was a series of messages, cryptic and coded, but with a thread of familiarity. "These messages," she said, her mind racing. "They remind me of something I saw in the encrypted files we found in the abandoned building."

Rahul nodded, his eyes gleaming with determination.

"I think we're getting closer to the mastermind. These messages might lead us to the person behind it all."

Their pursuit of the mastermind led them down a convoluted path, a journey that took them through a virtual maze of false identities and hidden servers. It was a dangerous game, and they understood that with each step, they risked exposing themselves to even greater danger. But they pressed on, their resolve unwavering. They were driven by a need for closure, by a burning desire to bring the mastermind to justice. They had come too far to turn back now.

As the days turned into weeks, their investigation reached a critical juncture. They had successfully traced the coded messages to a username – "CipherMaster." It was a moniker that sent shivers down their spines, a name that carried an air of authority and power in the dark corners of the web. Anjali and Rahul knew that they were on the right track. CipherMaster held the key to unravelling the entire syndicate, to exposing the person who had orchestrated the web of crimes that had plagued the city.

Their pursuit of CipherMaster led them to a remote location, a safe house they had established to shield themselves from prying eyes. It was a place where they could work undisturbed, a sanctuary where they could delve deeper into the digital world that held the answers they sought.

Sitting in the dimly lit room, their laptops humming with activity, Rahul's fingers flew across the keyboard. He was determined to trace CipherMaster's digital footprint, to unveil the person's true identity. Anjali, meanwhile, was on the phone with their trusted contacts in law enforcement, coordinating their efforts. She had shared their findings with them, and they were ready to move in as soon as they had a location. Hours turned into days as they worked tirelessly, following the digital breadcrumbs that would lead them to CipherMaster's lair. It was a race against time, a high-stakes battle of wits in the virtual realm.

And then, one fateful night, as the clock ticked past midnight, Rahul froze. "I've got it," he exclaimed, his voice trembling with excitement. Anjali leaned in to see what he had found. On the screen was a location – an IP address that traced back to a physical address in the city. It was the breakthrough they had been waiting for. Anjali immediately relayed the information to their contacts in law enforcement, setting the stage for the final confrontation. The raid was set in motion, a carefully coordinated operation to capture CipherMaster and bring an end to the syndicate's reign of terror.

As they waited for the operation to unfold, Anjali and Rahul knew that this was the moment they had been working towards. It was a moment of reckoning, a culmination of their relentless pursuit of justice.

The raid was a resounding success. CipherMaster was apprehended, and the syndicate's operations were dealt a crippling blow. The city breathed a collective sigh of relief, and Anjali and Rahul were hailed as heroes. But for them, the victory was bittersweet. They had exposed the mastermind, but they had also put themselves in the crosshairs of the most dangerous criminals in the city. Their lives were forever changed, and their safety was forever compromised.

As they looked out over the city, now bathed in the soft glow of a new day, Anjali and Rahul had faced the tangled webs of deception and emerged stronger, but the scars of their battle would remain with them forever.

Conflicting Emotions

The days following their narrow escape in the alleyway were a whirlwind of activity for Anjali and Rahul. Their investigation into the cybercrimes gripping Bangalore had intensified, and the boundaries between their professional and personal lives began to blur. They were no longer just colleagues; they were a team, bonded by shared danger and a mutual goal. But, as they were about to learn, some bonds are tested in the fires of revelation.

It was a late evening in Bangalore, and the city was alive with its usual cacophony of sounds and lights. Anjali and Rahul found themselves in her small, cluttered apartment, poring over documents and digital records, trying to piece together the intricate puzzle of the cybercrimes that had gripped the city. The air was heavy with the scent of spiced tea and the tension of unsaid words.

Anjali couldn't shake the nagging thought that had been bothering her since their visit to the old library. The name in the newspaper clipping, the one that had elicited such a subtle yet telling reaction from Rahul, was a thread that demanded to be pulled. She knew she had to confront him, despite the unease it caused her.

"Rahul," she began, her voice hesitant, "back at the library, the name we came across in the old article... I saw your reaction. It means something to you, doesn't it?"

Rahul's fingers stilled on the laptop keyboard. He didn't look at her, his gaze fixed on the screen. The silence stretched between them, thick and heavy.

"Anjali, let's just focus on the investigation," he replied, his voice even, but Anjali could hear the undercurrent of tension. She pressed on, her journalistic instincts refusing to let the matter rest.

"Rahul, if there's something in your past that's connected to all this, I need to know. We can't afford any secrets between us, not with what's at stake."

Finally, Rahul looked up, his eyes meeting hers. There was a storm brewing in them, a tumult of emotions he was struggling to keep at bay.

"My past has nothing to do with this," he said tersely, but Anjali could tell he wasn't being entirely truthful. The air in the room felt charged, the unspoken truths creating a barrier that hadn't been there before. Anjali's mind raced, piecing together the fragments of information, the cryptic reactions, and the guarded looks. It was clear that Rahul's past was a puzzle piece in this intricate game they were playing.

"Rahul, I trust you," Anjali said softly, her voice earnest. "But this... this wall you've put up, it's only going to make things harder for both of us. Whatever it is, we can face it together."

Rahul turned away, a muscle twitching in his jaw. "Some things are better left in the past, Anjali," he said, his voice barely above a whisper. "Trust me on this."

The conversation ended there, but the questions lingered, hanging in the air like a spectre. The night progressed, their work continuing in silence, but the easy camaraderie they had built was now tainted with doubt and uncertainty. As Anjali lay in bed later that night, staring at the ceiling, her mind was a tumult of thoughts. Rahul's past was a missing piece in a puzzle that was growing more complex by the day. She knew that to uncover the truth behind the cybercrimes, she would have to uncover the truth about Rahul.

Outside, Bangalore slept, oblivious to the turmoil brewing in the small apartment. The city of lights and shadows continued its eternal dance, just as Anjali and Rahul continued theirs - a dance of truth and trust, each step leading them further into the heart of the mystery. Their journey had taken an unexpected turn, and they were about to discover that some bonds are tested in the fires of revelation, and some truths are better left uncovered.

In the days that followed, Anjali couldn't shake the feeling of unease that had settled over their partnership. It was as if a rift had formed between them, a shadow cast by the secrets Rahul held close to his chest. They continued to work tirelessly on the cybercrime investigation, chasing leads and analyzing data, but their conversations outside of work were marked by palpable tension.

As the sun dipped below the Bangalore skyline, casting a warm orange glow across the city, Anjali decided to broach the subject once more. She couldn't bear the weight of the unspokenness any longer. They were sitting on Anjali's small balcony, sipping tea as the sounds of the bustling city faded into the background. The air was filled with the scent of blooming jasmine, a stark contrast to the heaviness that had settled between them.

"Rahul," Anjali began, her voice soft but resolute, "we can't continue like this. We're partners, and we need to trust each other completely. I can sense that something from your past is intertwined with this case, and it's affecting us."

Rahul sighed, his gaze fixed on the distant city lights. "Anjali, you're right. I should have been more upfront with you from the beginning."

Anjali leaned forward, her eyes searching his. "Tell me. Whatever it is, we'll face it together."

Rahul took a deep breath, and the weight of his past seemed to settle on his shoulders. "The name we found in the library, the one that triggered my reaction, it's connected to an old case. A case that haunted me for years."

Anjali listened intently as Rahul began to recount the story he had kept hidden. Years ago, he had been part of a different investigative team, one that had been chasing a notorious cybercriminal known as "Cipher." This criminal had orchestrated elaborate cyber heists, leaving behind a trail of destruction and stolen wealth. But what had haunted Rahul the most was the personal connection to Cipher.

The criminal's real name was Karthik, and he had been Rahul's best friend in college. They had shared dreams of changing the world through technology, but somewhere along the way, Karthik had fallen into the dark world of cybercrime. Rahul had tried to save his friend, but Karthik had eluded capture, and the case had gone cold.

Anjali sat in stunned silence as Rahul's story unfolded. The pieces of the puzzle were falling into place. Cypher was back, and he was wreaking havoc on Bangalore. But more importantly, Anjali now understood why Rahul had been so reticent about his past. It was a painful scar that he had tried to bury.

"I had no idea, Rahul," Anjali whispered, her voice filled with empathy.

Rahul nodded, his eyes clouded with regret. "I kept it hidden because I didn't want my past to cloud our judgment or put you in danger. But now that you know, we have to catch him. We have to bring Karthik to justice."

Anjali reached out and placed a reassuring hand on Rahul's shoulder. "We will, Rahul. Together."

From that moment on, their partnership shifted. They were no longer just investigators; they were two people with a shared mission, fueled by a determination to confront their pasts and protect their city. The tension between them dissipated, replaced by a newfound trust that bound them even closer together.

Days turned into weeks, and Anjali and Rahul relentlessly pursued Cipher's trail. The cybercriminals had left behind a complex web of digital footprints, but with their combined skills and determination, they were closing in. The chase led them through a labyrinth of virtual mazes and hidden identities, and each step brought them closer to unmasking the elusive Karthik.

Finally, one fateful night, their persistence paid off. Anjali and Rahul tracked Cipher to a hidden lair, deep within the city's digital underbelly. As they confronted him, a fierce battle of wits and technology ensued. It was a showdown that tested their skills, their resolve, and their bond. In the end, Anjali and Rahul emerged victorious. Karthik, the once brilliant friend turned criminal mastermind, was brought to justice. The city of Bangalore breathed a sigh of relief, knowing that the cybercrime wave had finally come to an end.

As they stood outside the police station, watching the officers lead Karthik away in handcuffs, Anjali turned to Rahul and smiled. "We did it, Rahul. We faced our pasts and emerged stronger."

Rahul smiled back, a sense of closure washing over him. "Yes, Anjali. And we did it together." Their journey had been a tumultuous one, marked by danger, secrets, and revelations. But through it all, Anjali and Rahul had discovered that some bonds are not only tested in the fires of revelation but also forged stronger, and that trust and truth are the pillars upon which the most formidable partnerships are built.

With Cipher behind bars, Anjali and Rahul returned to their daily lives, but the experience had left an indelible mark on both of them. Their partnership had evolved into something more profound, a deep bond forged in the crucible of adversity. As they continued to work together on other cases, their trust in each other only grew stronger.

Over time, their small, cluttered apartment became a hub of investigation, and the scent of spiced tea lingered in the air as they pored over new challenges. They tackled cybercrimes with renewed vigour, a united front against the threats that lurked in the digital shadows. But it wasn't just their professional lives that had changed. Anjali and Rahul found solace in each other's company outside of work, sharing moments of laughter, support, and even vulnerability. The walls that had once divided them had crumbled, and they were now a team in every sense of the word.

One evening, as they sat on the same balcony where they had confronted Rahul's past, Anjali spoke, breaking the comfortable silence that had settled between them. "Rahul, I'm glad we faced our pasts together. It brought us closer, and I feel like we can handle anything now."

Rahul nodded a genuine smile on his face. "Anjali, you've been my rock through all of this. I couldn't have asked for a better partner or friend." Their connection had grown beyond the confines of their professional lives, and they both knew it. But with that realization came a new set of questions and uncertainties.

Anjali took a deep breath, her gaze locked with Rahul's. "Rahul, there's something else I need to say. This journey has changed us, and I can't deny that I've developed feelings for you. I just wanted you to know."

Rahul's eyes widened in surprise, and he looked deeply into Anjali's eyes. "Anjali, I've been feeling the same way. I just didn't know how to bring it up." Their words hung in the air, a confession that had been a long time coming. As the city lights shimmered in the background, they leaned closer to each other, their lips meeting in a gentle kiss. It was a moment that sealed their bond, not just as partners but as lovers.

From that day forward, Anjali and Rahul faced not only the challenges of the cyberworld but also the complexities of their newfound relationship. They navigated the intricacies of love with the same determination and trust that had defined their partnership, and they found that their connection only deepened with each passing day.

The city continued to evolve, its lights and shadows dancing in a timeless rhythm. Anjali and Rahul, too, continued their dance, one that was now fueled by love, trust, and a shared commitment to truth and justice. Their journey had been a rollercoaster of revelations, but in the end, it had led them to a place where they had discovered not only the truth about the cybercrimes but also the truth about themselves and the unbreakable bond they shared.

Uncharted Waters

The sun dipped below the horizon, casting a warm orange glow across the city of Bangalore, signalling the end of another long day. Anjali and Rahul had just finished a gruelling session at the cybercrime unit's office, where they had been working on a particularly tricky case involving a network of hackers targeting financial institutions.

As they left the office together, the atmosphere was filled with a sense of accomplishment. They had cracked the case wide open, and the hackers would soon be brought to justice. The relief was palpable, and their smiles mirrored their mutual satisfaction. Outside, the bustling city seemed to buzz with energy, but Anjali and Rahul felt a sudden shift in the air as if something were about to change. The moment was charged with unspoken anticipation, and they exchanged a knowing glance.

"Rahul," Anjali began, her voice tinged with curiosity, "I can't help but wonder what's next for us. We've tackled some of the toughest cases together, and I can't imagine working with anyone else."

Rahul nodded, a thoughtful expression on his face. "You're right, Anjali. We've come a long way since that alleyway, and I couldn't have asked for a better partner, both personally and professionally."

Anjali took a deep breath, gathering her courage. "Rahul, what if we take the next step? What if we start our own private investigation agency? We have the skills, the experience, and the trust in each other. It could be the adventure of a lifetime."

Rahul's eyes sparkled with excitement as he considered her proposal. "Anjali, that's an intriguing idea. Starting our own agency would give us the freedom to choose our cases, work on what truly matters to us, and make a real impact." The prospect of embarking on a new journey together filled them with a sense of exhilaration. They began to envision the possibilities, from selecting their first case to building a team of skilled investigators. It was a dream that felt within reach.

As days turned into weeks, Anjali and Rahul put their plan into action. They rented a small office space in the heart of Bangalore, named it *"Sherlock Investigations,"* set up their investigative equipment, and started reaching out to potential clients. The response was overwhelming, and it seemed that their reputation as top-notch investigators had preceded them.

Their first case at Sherlock Investigations involved a missing person, a distraught mother searching for her teenage daughter who had disappeared without a trace. Anjali and Rahul dove into the investigation, utilizing their skills in cyber forensics, surveillance, and interviews. The case led them down a labyrinth of twists and turns, as they uncovered hidden secrets and unexpected allies. They worked tirelessly, chasing leads across the city and late into the night, never losing hope of reuniting the mother and daughter.

As they closed in on a breakthrough, their partnership was put to the test once more. The trial led to a high-profile tech company, where the missing teenager had been working undercover. The company's CEO, a powerful and influential figure, used his resources to thwart Anjali and Rahul's investigation.

The situation grew tense as they faced not only professional obstacles but also personal threats. Yet, their determination remained unshaken. Anjali and Rahul knew that they had to navigate these uncharted waters together.

One night, as they sat in their dimly lit office, pouring over evidence and formulating their next move, Anjali turned to Rahul. "Rahul, this case is pushing us to our limits, but we can't back down. We've come too far, and we owe it to our client." Rahul nodded in agreement. "You're right, Anjali. We'll confront this head-on. But we have to be prepared for whatever challenges lie ahead."

The days that followed were a relentless battle of wits, as they outsmarted the CEO's attempts to thwart their investigation. Their determination, coupled with their unwavering trust in each other, proved to be an unstoppable force.

As they closed in on the truth, they uncovered a network of corruption within the tech company, and the missing teenager's life hung in the balance. In a high-stakes showdown, they confronted the CEO, and justice prevailed as the truth came to light.

The missing teenager was safely reunited with her mother, and the corrupt CEO faced the consequences of his actions. Anjali and Rahul's private investigation agency had achieved its first major victory, and their reputation soared. As they stood on the rooftop of their office building, gazing out at the city lights, Anjali and Rahul shared a moment of quiet reflection. They had embarked on this journey together, faced uncharted waters, and emerged stronger than ever. Their partnership had evolved into something even more profound, and the adventure of a lifetime was just beginning.

Their decision to start Sherlock Investigations marked the beginning of a new chapter in Anjali and Rahul's lives. With boundless enthusiasm, they dove headfirst into the intricacies of entrepreneurship, transforming their small office space into a bustling hub of investigation.

The office, once a nondescript room, came alive with the hum of computers, the flickering of screens, and the constant chatter of their dedicated team of investigators. Anjali and Rahul had handpicked their team, ensuring that each member brought unique skills and expertise to the table. Together, they formed a close-knit family of truth-seekers, each fueled by a shared passion for uncovering secrets and solving mysteries.

Anjali and Rahul's workdays extended well into the night as they tackled cases ranging from missing persons to corporate espionage. Their private agency became known for its dedication to cases that others deemed unsolvable. They were driven by their unwavering belief in justice and their relentless pursuit of the truth. One evening, as they huddled around a conference table strewn with case files, Anjali couldn't help but marvel at how far they had come. "Rahul," she said, her voice tinged with a sense of pride, "Sherlock Investigations is more than I could have ever imagined. We've built something incredible together."

Rahul, his gaze fixed on a particularly challenging case file, nodded in agreement. "Anjali, it's a testament to our partnership and the trust we share. We've created a team that's making a real difference in people's lives." Their conversation was interrupted by the sound of a ringing phone.

Rahul answered it with a greeting, saying, "Hi, Rahul from Sherlock Investigations, How can I help you?" Their next case was set in motion. It was a case that would test their skills, their resolve, and their bond like never before. The case involved a missing person, a young woman named Maya who had vanished under mysterious circumstances. Her distraught family had turned to Anjali and Rahul for help, believing that only their expertise could bring her home.

Maya's disappearance was shrouded in intrigue. She had been a brilliant computer scientist working on cutting-edge technology. Her groundbreaking research had attracted the attention of both corporate giants and government agencies, and it was rumoured that her work held the key to a scientific breakthrough that could change the world. Anjali and Rahul's investigation led them into a complex web of corporate rivalries, international espionage, and a race to control Maya's research. They delved into her past, interviewing colleagues, friends, and family members, searching for any clue that might lead them to her whereabouts. Their journey took them from the bustling streets of Bangalore to remote research facilities in the mountains, as they followed a trail of breadcrumbs that seemed to lead to a world-changing discovery. With each step, they uncovered Maya's brilliance, her passion for her work, and the dangerous forces that sought to exploit her knowledge.

One rainy evening, as they sat in a dimly lit café, poring over stacks of documents and photographs, Anjali couldn't shake the feeling that they were on the cusp of a major breakthrough. "Rahul," she began, her voice filled with determination, "we're closing in on Maya's location, I can feel it."

Rahul, his brow furrowed in concentration, nodded in agreement. "Anjali, we've come too far to give up now. We'll follow this lead to the end and bring Maya back to her family."

Their relentless pursuit led them to a remote research facility hidden deep in the mountains, where Maya had been held against her will. The facility was guarded by a private security force with orders to protect Maya's research at all costs. In a tense standoff, Anjali and Rahul confronted the security team, demanding Maya's release. It was a moment of high tension, as they faced off against armed guards who were prepared to defend their secrets. But Anjali and Rahul's unwavering resolve and their reputation as relentless investigators ultimately prevailed.

As Maya emerged from the facility, her eyes filled with relief and gratitude, Anjali and Rahul knew that they had achieved another significant victory. They had reunited a family, uncovered a sinister plot, and protected Maya's groundbreaking research from falling into the wrong hands.

Back in Bangalore, Maya's safe return was celebrated by her family and their team of investigators. Anjali and Rahul had once again proven that they were a force to be reckoned with, and their private investigation agency's reputation continued to soar.

As they stood together on the rooftop of their office building, looking out at the city lights, Anjali and Rahul shared a moment of quiet reflection. Their journey had taken them through uncharted waters once more, but their partnership had remained steadfast.

"Anjali," Rahul said, his voice filled with gratitude, "Sherlock Investigations has become a beacon of hope for those in need. I couldn't be prouder of what we've accomplished together."

Anjali smiled, her heart filled with a sense of fulfilment. "Rahul, I can't wait to see where it takes us next. We're making a real difference in the world."

Their partnership had weathered the storms of their investigations, and they knew that many more mysteries were waiting to be uncovered. The world of private investigations was vast and ever-changing, but with their unwavering trust in each other, Anjali and Rahul were ready to navigate these uncharted waters, hand in hand.

Bonds Tested

With every successfully closed case, Sherlock Investigations grew stronger, and Anjali-Rahul's reputation as an elite investigator continued to spread like wildfire. Their once-modest office space had transformed into a bustling hub of activity, with a dedicated team of investigators working tirelessly to unearth hidden truths.

Their partnership had transcended the boundaries of a professional relationship. It had become an unbreakable bond, forged through countless challenges, the unravelling of mysteries, and daring confrontations with danger. Anjali and Rahul were no longer just colleagues; they had evolved into confidants, partners, and, most importantly, steadfast friends. As Sherlock's workload steadily increased, Anjali and Rahul often found themselves working late into the night. They shared dinners in the dimly lit office, and weekends were spent travelling to various parts of the country in pursuit of cases. These shared experiences nurtured a deep camaraderie, and they treasured the moments they stole away from their demanding work.

Yet, as their partnership grew stronger, so did the complexities of their relationship. Anjali couldn't shake the nagging thought that had haunted her since their visit to the old library. The name in the newspaper clipping, the one that had triggered Rahul's subtle yet telling reaction, had become a persistent thorn in her mind. She knew it was time to confront him, despite the unease it caused her.

One evening, in the hushed confines of their office, Anjali resolved to initiate the conversation she had been avoiding for too long. She turned to Rahul, her voice wavering but resolute, "Rahul, back at the library, the name we came across in the old article... I saw your reaction. It holds significance for you, doesn't it?"

Rahul's fingers paused on the laptop keyboard. He didn't meet her gaze, keeping his eyes locked on the computer screen. The silence that stretched between them was weighty, heavy with unspoken tension. "Anjali, let's stay focused on the investigation," he replied, his tone measured, but the underlying unease was palpable.

Determined to uncover the truth, Anjali pressed on, her journalistic instincts propelling her forward. "Rahul, if there's something from your past that's connected to our current work, I need to know. We can't afford to harbour secrets, not with so much at stake."

At last, Rahul turned to face her, his eyes revealing the emotional turmoil within. "My past has no bearing on this case," he responded tersely, though it was evident that he was withholding information.

The room seemed charged with unspoken truths, a previously unexperienced tension hung in the air. Anjali's mind raced, piecing together fragments of information, cryptic reactions, and guarded expressions. She understood that Rahul's past was an integral part of the complex puzzle they were trying to solve.

"Rahul, I trust you," she said, her voice gentle and sincere. "But this barrier you've erected will only make our path more treacherous. Whatever it is, we can confront it together."

Rahul looked away, his jaw twitching with internal conflict. "Some things are better left in the past, Anjali," he whispered, his voice barely audible. "Trust me on this."

Their conversation concluded, but the unresolved questions still loomed overhead, casting a shadow over their once-effortless partnership. The night wore on, work continued in silence, and the easy camaraderie they had shared now seemed tainted by doubt and uncertainty.

As Anjali lay in bed that night, her eyes fixed on the ceiling, her mind buzzed with tumultuous thoughts. Rahul's past was an elusive puzzle piece, intricately connected to the ever-evolving enigma of the cybercrimes they were striving to decipher. She understood that uncovering the truth behind these crimes meant she would have to unearth the buried secrets of Rahul's past, no matter how uncomfortable or unsettling they might be.

The days that followed their tense conversation were marked by a palpable tension between Anjali and

Rahul. Their once-seamless partnership now carried the weight of unspoken secrets, and each case they worked on seemed to bring them closer to the truth about Rahul's past.

Their office, once a place of camaraderie and shared victories, now felt like a battleground of unspoken emotions. The investigations continued, but a rift had formed, a chasm that neither of them knew how to bridge. Each day that passed without resolution deepened the unease that hung between them.

One evening, as they sat in their office, the air heavy with the unspoken, Anjali couldn't contain her frustration any longer. She pushed aside the case files in front of her and turned to Rahul. "Rahul, we can't keep avoiding this. We need to address what's going on between us. It's affecting our work, our partnership."

Rahul sighed, his expression weary. He looked like a man carrying the weight of the world on his shoulders. "Anjali, I told you, there are things in my past that I'm not proud of. Things I've been trying to leave behind. But it's not that simple."

Anjali leaned forward, her voice gentle but insistent. "Rahul, we're a team. We face challenges together, no matter how difficult. Whatever it is, we'll find a way to deal with it, but I can't help you if you don't open up."

Rahul hesitated, his gaze fixed on the floor. "It's not just about me, Anjali. It's about the people I've hurt, and the mistakes I've made. I've been trying to make amends, but it's not that easy."

Anjali reached out and placed a reassuring hand on his shoulder. "Rahul, we all make mistakes. What matters is how we choose to move forward. You're not alone in this."

With a heavy sigh, Rahul finally relented. He began to share his story, a story of a troubled past, of choices that had led him down a dark path, and of a relentless pursuit of redemption. Anjali listened intently, her heart going out to him, as he revealed the secrets he had kept hidden for so long.

Rahul's story was a tapestry of regret and resilience, woven with threads of sorrow and hope. Anjali learned about the decisions that had haunted him, the consequences that had shaped his present, and the constant battle he waged to set things right. It was a tale of a man striving to find his way back to the light, no matter how deep the shadows of his past.

As Rahul's narrative unfolded, Anjali realized that his past was indeed connected to their current investigations. The cybercrimes they were uncovering had ties to events from years ago, events that Rahul had been trying to distance himself from. The realization sent shockwaves through their partnership, but it also brought clarity to the cases they were working on.

The cybercrimes were not just random acts of hacking; they were orchestrated by individuals seeking revenge and using Rahul's past as leverage. Anjali understood that uncovering the truth about Rahul's past was not only a personal journey for him but also a vital step in solving the complex web of crimes they were entangled.

Their investigations led them to a shadowy figure from Rahul's past, a man named Vikram who held a deep-seated grudge against him. Vikram had orchestrated the cybercrimes as a means of exacting revenge, using the secrets from Rahul's history as a weapon. He was a formidable adversary, and their pursuit of him became a relentless game of cat and mouse.

Anjali and Rahul's partnership was put to the test once again as they faced the dual challenges of solving the cybercrimes and confronting Rahul's past. They relied on their trust in each other, their combined skills, and their unwavering determination to outsmart Vikram and dismantle his criminal network.

In a climactic showdown, they cornered Vikram, exposing his crimes and his motivations. With the evidence they had gathered, they ensured that he would face the consequences of his actions. It was a bittersweet victory, as they realized that the shadows of the past would always linger, but they had faced them together and emerged stronger.

That chapter ended with Anjali and Rahul standing together on the rooftop of their office building, gazing out at the city lights. Their journey had taken them through uncharted waters once more, but their partnership had remained steadfast. They had confronted their pasts, sought justice, and emerged as a stronger team. "Anjali," Rahul said, his voice filled with gratitude, "you've shown me that true strength lies in facing our past and making amends. I couldn't have asked for a better partner and friend."

Anjali smiled, her heart filled with a sense of closure. "Rahul, our bond has been forged in fire, and it's unbreakable. We've uncovered the truth, sought justice, and faced the shadows of our past. Our journey continues, and I can't wait to see what the future holds."

Shadows Lifted

In the wake of their confrontation with Vikram and the resolution of Rahul's past, a profound shift occurred in Anjali and Rahul's partnership. The unspoken tension that had once clouded their relationship had dissipated, replaced by a newfound sense of understanding and trust.

Sherlock Investigations continued to flourish, and the cases that came their way became even more complex and demanding. The challenges they faced were formidable, but their unwavering resolve and strengthened bond allowed them to tackle each obstacle with unwavering determination.

As the days turned into weeks, their office buzzed with activity. The team of investigators they had assembled worked seamlessly, their collective skills and dedication a testament to the agency's success. Anjali and Rahul took pride in mentoring their team and sharing their knowledge and experience to shape the next generation of elite investigators. Despite their busy schedules, Anjali and Rahul made it a point to set aside time for themselves. They realized the importance of maintaining the personal connection that had brought them together in the first place. Dinners in their favourite restaurants walks in the park, and quiet moments on their office rooftop allowed them to cherish their friendship outside the realm of investigations.

One evening, as they sat in their cosy office, a gentle breeze wafting through the open window, Anjali turned to Rahul with a reflective look. "Rahul, it's incredible how far we've come. Our journey has been filled with challenges, and yet, it's brought us here." Rahul nodded, a soft smile gracing his face. "Anjali, I couldn't agree more. Our partnership has evolved into something extraordinary, and I'm grateful for every moment we've shared."

Anjali's gaze turned thoughtful. "You know, Rahul, I've been thinking about the future. We've built something remarkable with Sherlock, and I can't help but wonder what lies ahead for us." Rahul's eyes sparkled with curiosity. "What are you getting at, Anjali?" She took a deep breath, her words measured and earnest. "What if we expand Sherlock, bring in more investigators, and take on even more challenging cases? We've proven ourselves time and again, and I believe we can make an even greater impact."

Rahul considered her proposal, his mind racing with possibilities. "Anjali, that's an intriguing idea. It would give us the opportunity to choose our cases, work on what truly matters to us, and make a real difference." The prospect of embarking on a new chapter in their partnership filled them with excitement. They began to discuss the logistics of expanding Sherlock, from finding a larger office space to recruiting talented investigators who shared their passion for justice.

Days turned into weeks, and their plan began to take shape. They rented a spacious office in a prime location, equipped with state-of-the-art technology and resources to support their growing team. The response to their recruitment drive was overwhelming, with experienced investigators eager to join Sherlock.

Their first case as an expanded agency involved a complex corporate espionage scheme that threatened to expose sensitive information about a major technology company. Anjali and Rahul, along with their team, delved into the investigation with their trademark tenacity and determination. The case led them on a journey through corporate boardrooms, encrypted servers, and underground hacker communities. They navigated a maze of deception, with the stakes higher than ever before. With each twist and turn, their partnership was tested, and each time, they emerged stronger, their trust in each other unshaken.

One night, as they gathered in their new office, poring over evidence and strategizing their next move, Anjali addressed the team. "This case is pushing us to our limits, but we can't back down. We've come too far, and we owe it to our client to see it through." Rahul nodded in agreement. "You're right, Anjali. We'll confront this head-on. But we have to be prepared for whatever challenges lie ahead."

The days that followed were a relentless battle of wits as they outsmarted the shadowy figures behind the corporate espionage scheme. As they closed in on the truth, they uncovered a network of corruption within the technology company, and the client's livelihood hung in the balance. In a high-stakes showdown, they confronted the mastermind behind the scheme, and justice prevailed as the truth came to light.

The victory was sweet, but it came at a cost. Anjali and Rahul had pushed themselves to their limits, and the toll on their physical and emotional well-being was evident. Sherlock Investigations had achieved its first major victory, and Anjali-Rahul's reputation soared, but they knew that the challenges they faced would only become more complex. As they stood on the rooftop of their new office building, gazing out at the city lights, Anjali and Rahul shared a moment of quiet reflection. They had embarked on this journey together, faced uncharted waters, and emerged stronger than ever. Their partnership had evolved into something even more profound, and the adventure of a lifetime was just beginning.

Sherlock Investigations became a beacon of hope for clients seeking justice. Anjali-Rahul's reputation as an elite investigator grew exponentially, drawing clients from all walks of life, each with their unique and often intricate cases. The new office, now a spacious and modern workspace, hummed with activity as their dedicated team of investigators worked tirelessly to uncover the truth. With each passing day, their partnership evolved into something even more profound. They had weathered countless challenges, solved mysteries, and faced danger head-on. Their personal and professional lives had become inseparable, their shared experiences forging an unbreakable bond that transcended mere colleagues. The lines between work and personal life blurred as they dedicated themselves to Sherlock's success. Late-night stakeouts shared dinners amidst stacks of case files, and weekends away on cases in far-flung locations became the norm. These moments, born from their commitment to justice, strengthened their connection and deepened their friendship.

The Final Confrontation

Sherlock Investigations had faced countless challenges, unravelling mysteries and confronting the shadows of the past. They had earned a reputation as a formidable force in the world of digital investigations. As they delved deeper into their cases, they couldn't help but feel that they were approaching a climax, a final confrontation that would test the limits of their partnership.

One fateful day, a case landed on their desk that would push them to their limits. It was a cyber threat unlike any they had encountered before. A group of highly skilled hackers had infiltrated critical infrastructure systems, threatening the stability and security of the nation.

As they delved into the investigation, it became clear that this was not just a random cyberattack. The hackers had a specific agenda, one that went beyond financial gain or political sabotage. Their motives were deeply personal, and their actions seemed to be driven by a vendetta against a particular individual.

Anjali and Rahul were determined to uncover the identity of the mastermind behind the cyberattacks and put an end to the threat. They delved into the digital realm, following a trail of encrypted codes and digital footprints, but the hackers proved to be elusive and highly sophisticated. The cybercriminals left cryptic messages, taunting Anjali and Rahul, and it became clear that they were playing a dangerous game. The stakes were higher than ever, and the nation's security hung in the balance.

Late one night, as they sat in their command centre, the glow of monitors casting eerie shadows on their faces, Anjali addressed the team. "This is the most critical case we've ever faced, and the threat is personal. We have to outsmart these hackers, no matter the cost. Lives and the security of our nation are at stake." Rahul nodded in agreement. "Anjali, we've come too far to back down now. We'll confront this head-on, just like we've always done."

Their determination fueled their efforts, and they worked tirelessly to uncover the hackers' identities. As they closed in on the truth, they discovered that the mastermind behind the cyberattacks had a deep-rooted connection to Rahul's past. The revelation sent shockwaves through their team, and Anjali couldn't help but feel a sense of déjà vu. The echoes of the past had returned, and it was clear that they were facing an adversary who had a personal vendetta against Rahul.

The final confrontation loomed, and Anjali and Rahul knew that they had to confront their adversary head-on. They relied on their trust in each other, their combined expertise, and their unwavering determination to navigate the treacherous digital landscape. In a high-stakes showdown, they tracked down the mastermind behind the cyberattacks, confronting their adversary in a virtual battlefield. The battle of wits and skill pushed them to their limits as they fought to protect the nation's security and uncover the truth.

As the battle raged on, the mastermind revealed their motives, a complex web of personal grievances and a desire for revenge. It became clear that this confrontation was not just about cybercrimes; it was about confronting the past and seeking closure.

Anjali and Rahul's partnership faced its greatest test yet as they grappled with the emotional and personal dimensions of the case. They had to make a choice — whether to let the shadows of the past continue to haunt them or to confront their adversary and seek justice.

In a climactic moment, Anjali and Rahul managed to outsmart the mastermind, exposing their identity and motives. The cyberattacks were thwarted, and the nation's security was safeguarded. Justice prevailed, but it came at a personal cost. As they stood together in the aftermath of the confrontation, Anjali and Rahul shared a moment of quiet reflection. Their journey had brought them full circle, and they had faced the shadows of the past head-on.

"Anjali," Rahul said, his voice filled with gratitude and weariness, "we've confronted the past and sought justice. Our partnership has been tested in ways we couldn't have imagined." Anjali smiled, her heart filled with a sense of closure and accomplishment. "Rahul, our bond is unbreakable, and our journey has been extraordinary. We've unravelled the mysteries of the past, and our partnership remains stronger than ever."

Their partnership had withstood the test of time, the challenges they had faced, and the shadows of the past. They knew that their journey was far from over, but with their unwavering trust and shared commitment to justice, Anjali and Rahul were ready to confront whatever lay ahead hand in hand, and heart to heart.

New Beginnings

The aftermath of the final confrontation left Anjali and Rahul with a sense of closure and a renewed sense of purpose. Sherlock Investigations had weathered the storm of cyber threats and personal vendettas, emerging stronger than ever. As they stood together in their office, surrounded by the glow of monitors and the hum of activity from their team, Anjali turned to Rahul. "Rahul, we've come a long way, and we've faced challenges that tested our partnership in unimaginable ways. But now, it feels like a new beginning."

Rahul nodded in agreement, a sense of determination in his eyes. "Anjali, our journey has brought us full circle, and it's time to chart a new course. We've proven that Sherlock Investigations can handle the toughest cases, and I believe we can achieve even more."

With that shared vision, Anjali and Rahul began to strategize the future of Sherlock. They discussed expanding their team, reaching out to new clients, and taking on cases that would make a lasting impact. Their expertise in cybercrime investigation had earned them a reputation that extended far beyond their city's borders.

Months passed, and Sherlock continued to thrive. They expanded their reach, taking on cases that ranged from international corporate espionage to high-profile missing persons investigations. Their team of investigators grew, each member sharing their commitment to uncovering the truth and seeking justice.

One evening, as they gathered in a café close to the office to celebrate another successful case, Anjali raised a toast. "To new beginnings and the endless possibilities of Sherlock."

Rahul smiled, clinking his cup of coffee against hers. "To our unwavering partnership and the difference we make in the world."

The remnants of the day's monsoon formed rivulets on the café windows, the steady drumming of raindrops creating a melancholic melody. The café was dimly lit, a silent witness to the burgeoning tension between them, a tension wrought by an unspoken attraction that had been building with each shared glance and subtle touch.

Their journey had taken them through uncharted waters, tested the limits of their partnership, and brought them face-to-face with the shadows of the past. But through it all, Anjali and Rahul had emerged as a formidable team, ready to face whatever challenges the future held. In a world where mysteries abound and justice is a beacon in the darkness, Anjali and Rahul stood as a formidable duo. Their journey together had been an extraordinary tapestry of new cases and enigmas, each one a thread interwoven into the fabric of their professional lives. Their bond, unbreakable and forged in the crucible of challenge, had always been the cornerstone of their partnership.

But as they faced the uncharted territories of future cases and clients, something profound and beautiful blossomed between them. It transcended the realms of partnership and friendship, touching the very essence of love and companionship.

With a voice that carried the weight of his sincere emotions, Rahul spoke of their journey together, of the challenges they had faced, and the victories they had celebrated. He talked about the depth of his respect for her, the joy she brought into his life, and how every moment with her was a treasure he cherished. Anjali's eyes, usually so full of fire and determination, now held a softness as she looked across the table at Rahul. There was a vulnerability there, a fear that the bond they had formed might unravel with the case's end. She took a deep breath, the air laden with the scent of rain-soaked earth and brewing coffee, a scent that would forever remind her of this moment, of this confession.

"I'm scared," she repeated, her voice a whisper that seemed too loud in the silence between them. "What if 'we' are just a product of this madness? What if what I feel…"

Rahul held her gaze, his own heart a tumultuous sea, mirroring the storm outside. He had always been the one with the plan, the one who charted the course through the dark waters of cybercrime. Yet now, faced with the tempest of Anjali's emotions, he found his composure slipping. "You're not alone in this fear," he said, his voice steady despite the turmoil within. "I too find myself wondering what lies beyond this storm. What happens when we're no longer chasing shadows?"

The question hung in the air, as heavy as the clouds outside. Anjali's fingers stopped their nervous dance along the table's edge, steadying as she took in Rahul's words. It was the first time he had voiced his doubts, the first time he had allowed her to see the man behind the mask of control.

"The truth is," Rahul continued, "I've come to rely on you, not just as a partner in this investigation, but as someone who…" He hesitated, the next words carrying the weight of his guarded heart. "Someone who has become essential to me."

Anjali's breath caught at his admission. She had seen glimpses of his guarded affection in stolen moments: a protective hand at the small of her back, a concerned gaze when she ventured too far into the danger, a smile that seemed meant only for her. But now, hearing the raw truth in his voice, she allowed herself to believe that what she felt was not a figment of her imagination.

"Rahul," she started, her voice firmer as she found her resolve. "I've been alone for so long, chasing stories, chasing the next big reveal. But with you, I've found something different, something that feels like… home."

The word hung between them, a fragile notion in their transient world. Rahul's hand reached across the table, his fingers brushing against hers, a touch that sent a jolt of electricity through them both. Anjali's hand turned beneath his, her palm meeting his in a silent acknowledgement of their connection.

"Home," Rahul echoed the simple word encapsulating the myriad emotions he had struggled to name. "You've become that for me too, Anjali. You've turned my solitary existence into something more, something worth fighting for beyond the bytes and code."

Outside, the rain began to let up, the relentless cascade slowing to a gentle patter. The café, with its soft jazz and hushed whispers, seemed to breathe a sigh of relief, the storm outside waning, as if in deference to the one unfolding within.

Anjali looked up, her eyes shining with unshed tears, not of sadness but of a profound recognition. "Rahul, I don't know what the future holds for us. But I do know that I no longer want to face it alone. Not when I've found someone who understands the silence between words, the stories behind the smiles, the pain behind the bravery."

Rahul's thumb caressed the back of her hand, a tender gesture that spoke louder than any promise. "Then let's not face it alone," he said. "Let's face it together, Anjali. Whatever comes, whatever we uncover, we'll do it side by side."

The promise was a beacon in the night, a light that cut through the remnants of the storm. They sat there, hands clasped, hearts open, as the café's clock ticked away the minutes. It was a scene etched in time, a moment of clarity amidst the chaos of their lives.

As the night deepened and the café's patrons dwindled, Rahul and Anjali remained in their haven, talking of everything and nothing, of fears and hopes, of the past and the future. Their conversation meandered like the winding streets of Bangalore, touching upon memories, pausing at dreams, and exploring the landscape of their joined paths.

When they finally stepped out into the cool night, the air fresh with the promise of a new beginning, they did so with a shared sense of purpose. The case that had brought them together was still there, its shadows still lurking in the corners of the city. But now, they had something more to fight for, a bond that had been forged in the heart of the code, in the heart of the storm.

After leaving the café, Anjali and Rahul walked silently, side by side, through the rain-washed streets of Bangalore. The city, rejuvenated by the monsoon showers, shimmered under the streetlights, its vibrant energy a stark contrast to the serene bubble that had enveloped them in the café. Anjali's thoughts swirled like the eddies of water on the pavement – her heart a tumultuous sea of emotions, waves of hope and fear crashing within her.

Rahul, sensing her inner turmoil, stopped and gently guided her to a quiet park they often passed during their investigations. The park, a lush oasis amidst the urban sprawl, was deserted at this hour, its usual bustle of families and joggers replaced by the symphony of crickets and the rustling of leaves.

Under a canopy of ancient trees, they found a secluded bench. The soft glow of the park lights created a cocoon of intimacy, the world beyond their reach for the moment. Rahul turned to face Anjali, taking her hands in his. His eyes, usually a well of strength and resolve, now shimmered with an unspoken question, a depth of feeling that Anjali had only seen glimpses of before.

"Anjali," he began, his voice a gentle caress in the night air. "From the moment we started working together, I knew you were someone extraordinary. You've challenged me, supported me, and stood by me through the darkest of times."

Anjali's heart fluttered, her breath catching at the tenderness in his words. The park around them faded into a blur, the only reality being the man before her, his soul laid bare under the starlit sky.

"With you, I've discovered a part of myself I thought was lost. You've brought light into my life, a light that I thought had extinguished long ago." Rahul's grip on her hands tightened, as if holding onto her was his anchor in a sea of uncertainty.

Anjali felt a tear escape her eye, tracing a warm path down her cheek. Rahul reached out, tenderly brushing it away with the pad of his thumb. "Anjali, I don't want to imagine a future without you. I want to share every triumph, every defeat, every mundane moment with you. I want to wake up every day knowing that you're by my side."

He knelt on one knee, his gaze never leaving hers, a symbol of his unwavering commitment. "Anjali Sharma, will you be my partner not just in this investigation, not just in the thrill of the chase, but in life? Will you marry me?"

The words hung in the air, a testament to the journey they had embarked upon together. Anjali, overwhelmed by the raw sincerity in his proposal, found herself at a loss for words. Her heart answered before her lips could, a resounding yes that echoed in the depths of her soul.

"Yes, Rahul," she whispered her voice a melody that intertwined with the chorus of the night. "Yes, I will marry you."

Rahul's face broke into a radiant smile, mirroring the joy that illuminated Anjali's features. He stood up, enveloping her in an embrace that spoke volumes of their shared past and the promise of their future. In his arms, Anjali felt a sense of belonging, a sense of coming home.

Around them, the park remained a silent witness to their love, the trees swaying gently as if in celebration. The night air was filled with the scent of rain-soaked earth and blooming flowers, nature itself rejoicing in their union.

As they held each other, the challenges ahead seemed surmountable, the shadows of their profession less daunting. They were two souls, once solitary, now bound by a love that transcended the codes and conspiracies that had brought them together.

The proposal in the heart of the park was a harbinger of a new beginning, a promise of a life filled with shared dreams and aspirations. They stood together, hand in hand, their hearts beating in unison, ready to embark on a journey not just of uncovering truths but of building a life together.

In the quiet of the park, under the canopy of stars, Anjali and Rahul found not just a resolution to their quest but a discovery of a deeper connection, a love that would guide them through whatever the future held. It was a moment etched in time, a memory that would be a beacon in their lives, illuminating their path as they stepped into the dawn of a new day, together.

Epilogue: To Love, Laughter & Happily Ever After..!!!

The vibrant hues of Bangalore were in full bloom as Anjali Sharma and Rahul Nair, united in a marriage that blended traditional rituals with their unique modern love story, embarked on a new journey together. Their wedding day, held in the lush gardens of Leela Palace, was a celebration that mirrored their journey - a perfect amalgamation of the city's rich heritage and the pulsating beat of its tech-driven heart.

As they stood hand in hand, surrounded by family, friends, and colleagues who had been part of their remarkable journey, Anjali and Rahul felt a deep sense of fulfilment. The air was filled with music, laughter, and an aura of love, setting the foundation for the new life they were about to build together.

Months into their marriage, the couple experienced a momentous joy that added a new dimension to their lives - Anjali's pregnancy! It was a journey filled with anticipation, excitement, and a touch of the nervous energy that comes with stepping into the unknown. Rahul, ever the pillar of support, was by her side, sharing in every moment, every milestone.

Their joy doubled when they welcomed not one, but two new lives into the world. The birth of their twins - Ayaan and Anaaya, was a moment that stood still in time, a precious memory etched in the heart of their family. The twins, with their first cries, brought a new kind of love into Anjali and Rahul's lives, a love that was profound and life-altering.

As Anjali and Rahul adjusted to their new roles as parents, their home became a haven of warmth, filled with the soft gurgles and laughter of their children. Each day brought new discoveries, new challenges, and new joys. The twins, with their distinct personalities, were a beautiful blend of their parents - Ayaan inheriting Rahul's quiet curiosity and Anaaya displaying Anjali's spirited charm. Life for the Nairs was a beautiful balance of professional pursuits and the joys of parenthood.

Sherlock Investigations continued to thrive under their leadership, tackling the complexities of cybercrime with the same zeal and dedication. Yet, now, there was a newfound purpose to their work - creating a safer world for their children to grow up in.

Standing on their balcony, watching the city lights twinkle against the night sky, Anjali and Rahul reflected on the journey that had led them here. They had faced challenges, both professionally and personally, but each hurdle had only strengthened their bond. Now, with their children by their side, they looked towards the future with hope and determination.

Their story was more than a tale of love and crime-solving in the digital age; it was a testament to the enduring power of family, partnership, and resilience. As they turned to join Ayaan and Anaaya, playing in the warmth of their living room, Anjali and Rahul knew that their adventure was merely evolving, growing richer with each passing day.

Their story, a saga of "Digital Love, Analog Hearts," continued to unfold, echoing with laughter, love, and the endless possibilities of the future!

About the Author

Sneha Sreekumar

Say hello to Sneha Sreekumar, living and loving life in the heart of Bangalore. She's more than just your average HR Leader – she's a standout, handling her day job with a grace and poise that's downright admirable. But here's where it gets interesting: Sneha's real passion is writing. For her, it's not just a hobby, it's where her heart sings and her soul finds its true voice. This, her first novel is like her imagination and creativity poured onto pages, a labor of love that's as heartfelt as it is beautiful.

At home, Sneha's world is full of warmth and laughter, thanks to her adorable four-year-old, Shresht, and her ever supportive husband, Sreenath. Their days are filled with little moments of joy, the regular nok-jhok of everyday life and the warmth of home-cooked meals. And everytime she needs a little me-time, Sneha heads to her cozy writing nook, where her imagination really takes flight.

Don't forget to check out her blog, "Unfilteredmusingsbysneha.blogspot.com." It's like a chat over coffee, packed with stories and experiences that are as real as they are touching.

Finishing her first novel is like a huge deal for her! It's like ticking off a big dream from her bucket list. Her journey's been all about letting her imagination and creativity shine, and guess what? She's just warming up. In her own words, *"I hope you're ready for my next story,"* and if it's anything like her first, we're in for a treat. So, keep an eye out – Sneha's stories are the kind that stick with you, long after the story ends.

www.ingramcontent.com/pod-product-compliance
Lightning Source LLC
LaVergne TN
LVHW041613070526
838199LV00052B/3122